FENN HALFLIN AND THE SEABORN

FENN HALFLIN AND THE SEABORN

Francesca Armour-Chelu

WALKER
BOOKS

First published in Great Britain 2017 by Walker Books Ltd
87 Vauxhall Walk, London SE11 5HJ

2 4 6 8 10 9 7 5 3 1

Text © 2017 Francesca Armour-Chelu
Map illustration © 2017 Francesca Armour-Chelu
Cover design © 2017 Richard Collingridge

This book has been typeset in Palantino

Printed and bound in Great Britain by Clays Ltd, St Ives plc

British Library Cataloguing in Publication Data:
a catalogue record for this book is available from the British Library

ISBN 978-1-4063-6618-1

www.walker.co.uk

For my children, Charlie, Sam and Rosa
With all my love

I

He should never have escaped. No one ever escaped.

Chilstone sat alone at the helm, staring into the surf far below as the *Warspite*'s bow split the iron-coloured waves like a cleaver. They had sailed clear of the remains of the Shanties six days before, but he could still see black splashes of tar bespattering the bow's stem, from when the *Warspite* had crashed through the burning sea-slum. Behind him stood the huge Scragnet, a new addition to the *Warspite*. A crane supported an arm and chain, from which hung an enormous magnet, bearing the Terra Firma logo of a black T and F against a scarlet background. Chilstone smiled at his latest improvement: the Scragnet was making the capture of the Seaborns' ships quicker and could also be fitted with a net to haul living Seaborns from the water. In Chilstone's eyes, anything that helped sweep up sea-vermin was a good thing.

The passing of time never faded his hatred of them.

Chilstone had been on deck all night, scouring the horizon for any sign of the boat that the boy had escaped on, but as usual there had been nothing. Tiredness made the skin on his face hang in deep folds as if he was starting to melt, but beneath, his jaw was clenched tight. A stabbing sensation shot through his legs where iron pegs anchored muscle to bone, and he shifted position to ease the agony. He winced as the feeling slithered up through the fibres of his body. Pain had dozed a little in the night, but now it was sharply awake.

You let it happen again, it muttered.

"Who said that?" Chilstone shouted, quickly pulling himself up from the wooden block he'd been resting on and looking around wildly.

But no one was there; the rain-lashed deck was completely empty – apart from pooling water and a scrap of rope at Chilstone's feet. Chilstone nudged it with the tip of his steel cane and stooped to pick it up, catching his breath as the pain unfurled up his back. In his hand he held a sort of doll, twisted from a piece of cord, the strands untwined to make arms and legs and knotted at the top to make a head. It must have belonged to one of the children who'd been brought up on deck. He was distracted from the pain for a few seconds, wondering which child it had belonged to, trying to remember their faces, but then the voice came closer, whispering in his ear.

If you don't catch him...

Chilstone tossed the little doll over the rail and clamped his hands over his ears, trying to block the voice out. Needing somewhere the voice wouldn't find him, he limped around the Scragnet, keeping a safe distance from its powerful magnet. Breathing hard, he got to the first gun turret, taking refuge in its shadow, hoping the voice hadn't followed. He stood in the shadows for several minutes and when he was sure he was alone, he tentatively lowered his hands, just for a second. That was the only chance the voice needed.

He's going to destroy...

"Shut up!" Chilstone shouted. "Shut up! I'll find him!"

He had been hunting the Demari child for over thirteen years now, ever since he had his parents killed, and he'd never got so close again. His spies reported the boy arriving on the Shanties, dumped by a ship called the *Panimengro*, one of the Gleaners that made the perilous treks between the scraps of remaining land. Chilstone couldn't be certain it was the same kid from East Marsh, but the description matched him well enough: dark-haired, tall, like his father, and the right age. The boy should have been scooped up in the Sweep, but instead he'd vanished into thin air, dissolving like the flecks of white surf below. It hadn't taken

Chilstone long to work out where that Gleaner had come from, or where it was going. Gleaners often crossed the Biscay Gulf, the enormous expanse of water between East Isle and West Isle, their holds stuffed with stinking flotsam one way, stinking Seaborns on their return. He knew exactly where the kid would go, what he'd do. He'd try to get to West Isle, where rumour had it Seaborns were welcomed. This was where the *Warspite* was now heading.

Dawn was breaking and the skies were purple-black like bruises. Chilstone limped back to the ship's rail and stared across the sea, explaining himself to the voice in his head. He and the voice often quarrelled with each other, but it helped Chilstone to talk things through with the one he could trust to always be by his side, his constant companion: the excruciating pain that time could not fade.

Standing there, arguing with himself, he didn't hear the real voices calling his name until too late. When he did, he stepped out from the gloom, quickly pulling his cowl up over his head to shield his face from scrutiny. He didn't like anyone looking at him.

Two Terras had brought a man up on deck. This prisoner was different; he'd begged to see Chilstone, had something to tell him. The man couldn't walk so the Terras had to drag him along between them, his feet sliding on the ground behind him like a mop, leaving a trail through the wet deck.

When they were still several feet away, Chilstone put his hand up and the three of them stopped abruptly. The older Terra – hardened by years at sea, his nose scabbed by harsh winds – pulled the man up sharply to a standing position, where he stood, swaying gently as if he was drunk. The Terra roughly shoved him in the ribs to pay attention to Chilstone, but the prisoner's head still lolled on his shoulders, so that a long shock of thin hair fell down in front of his eyes. Chilstone put out his cane and lifted the strands away so he could see the prisoner clearly.

He sighed. The man's eyes were as puffy and shiny as damson plums. Hadn't he expressly told the Terras not to beat them on the face? It was hard to tell if someone was lying when you couldn't see their eyes, and it was just as effective to beat hands or feet when you wanted answers. But even if the prisoner was a mess, it was still clear to Chilstone that this was no ordinary Shanties dweller; he was plumper than the usual bags of bones the Terras had hauled up on deck over the past few days.

"You have something to tell me?" Chilstone enquired.

The man tried to speak, but only managed to slur inaudibly.

"Speak up!" Chilstone demanded. The old Terra jabbed the man in the stomach again and this time he straightened up, mumbling. Chilstone gestured to the blood gluing the man's lips together.

The other Terra, new to his post, took a cloth from his pocket, soaked it in the pooling water on the deck and gingerly rubbed it over the prisoner's mouth, trying not to hurt him. Not every Terra was the same. The prisoner cautiously parted and stretched his lips, as if testing the efficiency of his damaged mouth.

"My name…" he croaked.

"Your name is unimportant—" Chilstone began but then the man did something no one had ever done to Chilstone. He interrupted him.

"Leach," he said. "Nile Leach. I know who you're looking for."

From the shadow of his cowl, Chilstone drew a low, hissing breath, trying to repress any sign that he cared about what Nile said.

They all say that, warned the voice in his head, but Chilstone couldn't resist his excitement.

"Who?"

Careful! the voice scolded.

"A boy … the Demari boy," Nile continued, peering into the deep shadows to find Chilstone's eyes; to see his reaction, to catch a sense of his feelings. But Chilstone was listening to the voice again and his eyes were lifeless once more. He cocked his head to one side, trying to catch Nile's words. It was hard for him to hear what people said with the voice constantly muttering in his ear.

"...a Gleaner ship dumped him; the *Panimengro*," Nile finished.

Nothing new here. You know all this already, the voice continued. *Another rumour-monger. Another time-waster.*

Chilstone gave up; the voice was right. It was always right. He nodded to the nearest Terra, who took hold of Nile's arm and tugged him over towards the bow. The Terra was tall and thickset, easily strong enough to deal with prisoners, even ones who struggled hard.

The *Warspite* had circled the Shanties like a shark until Chilstone was certain all the inhabitants were either drowned or in the *Warspite*'s hold. The Scragnet had netted six hundred and fifteen survivors, hoisting them up the *Warspite*'s side before emptying the human haul out on deck, like a catch of fish. Obviously a few always drowned in the net – that couldn't be helped – but at roll call the day before, only five hundred and ninety were counted.

Chilstone personally oversaw twenty or so interrogations, trying to find out what had become of the Demari boy. All the prisoners had tried to improve their circumstances by claiming to have information about the last Demari. Men had attempted to bargain their way on to one of the Labour-Ships where they hoped to escape to freedom, and women had pleaded for their children to be allowed to work as servants on one of the Isles.

But none told Chilstone anything he didn't already know; nothing that wasn't woven into the fabric of the myth he was determined to destroy. Not one of them verified a unique piece of evidence that could convince him that Maya's child had definitely survived all those years ago. Not even as they braced themselves for the hundred-foot drop off the *Warspite's* bow, weeping and making stuff up to save their skins. None of it led Chilstone any nearer to his prey. The only surprise for Chilstone was that Seaborns should have such affection for their miserable lives, and would go to such lengths to keep hold of them.

The older Terra shoved Nile towards the block where Chilstone had been sitting. It was only when Nile saw the bolt on the deck rail and the other Terra pulling it back that he realised what was about to happen.

"Wait!" Nile yelled, struggling to break loose. "Fenn!" he shouted. "Fenn!"

The voice stopped muttering in Chilstone's ear, suddenly expectant. *A name?* it hissed hopefully.

Chilstone looked at Nile with sharp interest and clicked his fingers, motioning the Terras to stop. Nile collapsed on the spot.

"Thank you, thank you!" he whispered. His voice was fragile, whittled thin by fear.

"Continue," Chilstone ordered.

"I never liked him," Nile began, trying to curry favour. "I took him in and he stole from me!" he complained. Chilstone's eyes narrowed in disapproval.

The son of the Demaris? A petty thief? the voice asked.

"Yes! Yes, he did!" Nile nodded sincerely, almost as if he could hear the murmurings in Chilstone's head too. He could tell Chilstone was a man of business like himself; he'd understand. "Gave him a home and he tricked me. Stole four of my employees. Two girls, two boys."

But Chilstone wasn't listening again – Nile could see that he'd lost him. Chilstone needed hard facts. Nile scoured his mind for what those might be.

Nile was cunning. In his time he'd been a con artist and a smuggler of goods and children. Before the Shanties he'd been imprisoned on a Hellhulk prison ship, in the days when they were only for criminals the Terras didn't want taking up room on land, and before they were packed with Seaborns to move from Isle to Isle. When the building started on the Walls that would protect the land from the rising waters, all criminals were sent to guard the Seaborn workforce.

Nile hadn't fancied that, so had jumped to freedom, been rescued by a Gleaner and feigned sickness to avoid work before being dumped at the Shanties. On the first night he'd befriended the previous owner of the precious fort – one of the few places you could go to sleep at the Shanties and be sure to wake up again. On the second night he'd murdered his new friend as he slept and took the fort for his own. You didn't do all that without having a nose for survival.

Nile had immediately recognised the hungry look in Chilstone's eyes when he heard Fenn's name. Chilstone obviously wanted more details.

"There was definitely something odd about him," Nile said tantalisingly. Chilstone seemed to take the bait as he leant in to hear. "His eyes were different colours," Nile continued.

A shiver ran up Chilstone's spine; the proof he'd been waiting for. He'd never been certain the child had inherited his mother's rare eye condition. But now there was another problem. How many Seaborns must the boy have met at the Shanties? If it were no longer a secret that the Demari boy was alive, there was no point in trying to pretend the Demari boy was just a myth any more. He'd need to give the Terras a clear description, so in the next Sweep they knew exactly who they were looking for. It was now a race to get to him first; if there was any Resistance left, they would want him as a figurehead. Chilstone needed to catch and kill him and put an end to the Resistance once and for all.

But can you be sure it's really him? whispered the voice in Chilstone's head.

"Was there anything else about him?" Chilstone asked. If the boy had the famous Demari key, he would have to get it. The symbol of the Resistance actually in his grasp? That would send out a powerful message to any more rebellious Seaborns out there.

"The kid kept on about his grandfather. Works the Punchlock on East Point. A man called Halflin."

Halflin! The old forger, working off his crimes against the Terra Firma by destroying Seaborns' boats in the Punchlock – a cruel punishment designed to break either the old man's heart or spirit. Chilstone stared back across the steely skies towards the rising sun. So Halflin had said he was his grandfather, had he? He should have dug deeper when he first questioned the old man thirteen years before about whether he'd found a child aboard the barge he'd sunk.

Chilstone remembered it well: Halflin staring into the fire, sweating and slurring his answers, an empty bottle in his fist. Chilstone smiled ruefully; so he'd been tricked? Halflin hadn't been drinking at all. He must have worked up that sweat by running; he must have hidden the baby on the marsh before racing back to set himself up to look like a drunk who'd been broken by the loss of his family and the daily horror of scuttling the Seaborns' boats. Chilstone had always suspected the old boat-breaker was craftier than he looked; an ignoramus who could scarcely spell his own name, yet forged papers so well his best Terras didn't spot them. But if Chilstone had underestimated Halflin, Halflin had underestimated Chilstone too. He must have thought Chilstone would forget eventually – a fatal mistake. Chilstone would never forget. In some ways it was a pity Halflin had died. He would have been more useful alive; they could have used him to lure the boy in.

"So your ship's going in the wrong direction," Nile finished as he battled to keep Chilstone's attention. Chilstone stared at Nile as he stood up, brushed himself down and stroked his hair back across his bald patch. "Fenn was heading back to East Marsh."

We've got all we need, muttered the voice impatiently. Chilstone smiled and turned to Nile.

"You've been helpful," he said as he nodded at the Terras again.

Immediately the older Terra wrenched Nile's arms behind his back, and thrust them roughly upwards so Nile staggered forwards. The other knocked back the bolt holding the rail in place and made an opening from the bow of the *Warspite* into the foaming waves below.

"But I told you everything!" Nile screamed in anguish. "Please, sir! I can help you find him. I know him! I know what he looks like!"

"Precisely," Chilstone said. "So I can't have you back down in the hold telling everyone what you know."

"I won't breathe a word!" Nile pleaded. "I promise! You can trust me. I'm Landborn. I'm like you!" he whimpered, clutching weakly at the guard's uniform. "I'll do anything! Let me work for you!" The guard gripped Nile's wrists, then yanked him towards the deck rail.

With a violent wriggle, Nile slipped out of his grasp and seized the rail, looping his arm through the bars and bunching his legs under his chin, like a child taking a go on a rope swing; anything to make it harder for the Terras to get hold of him. But he was weak and they prised him away easily.

Chilstone didn't even bother to watch as the Terras pushed Nile overboard and bolted back the rail. He never thought it would, but the novelty of watching them fall had worn off very quickly.

"Turn the ship," he commanded as Nile's screams faded.

2

The sun had dropped behind a thick grey bank of cloud and the air had chilled. Fenn poked another stick into the fire's heart, making a fountain of sparks, before gulping down another dollop of the stew Amber had cooked. It tasted just like the dish Magpie had made for him on his first night aboard the *Panimengro* when he'd fled East Marsh, leaving his grandad behind.

"Amber told us to turn back," Fathom continued as he handed Gulper a bowl. Gulper began to slurp noisily and gave Amber a friendly prod in the ribs.

"So what if I did? We couldn't leave you!" she protested, smiling at Fenn while she licked her spoon.

The stew's flavours melted onto Fenn's tongue like smoke and he tried to remember the name Magpie had given it. Suddenly it darted back into his mind: Gumbo. He missed

Magpie and her food and wondered where she was now. He had no idea Amber could cook so well or what she'd used to make the food taste so good. Perhaps she'd taken some spices from the *Salamander* when they moored the old barge in the flooded barn at Hill Farm.

"My mammi used to make this," Comfort whispered shyly in Fenn's ear as Fathom ladled some stew into her bowl. At the same moment, Fenn noticed how Amber was peering at him quizzically. In fact all his friends were looking at him with surprise. Amber took the spoon out of her mouth and said, "Something's wrong, isn't it? When did Comfort start talking? And why are you eating stew in bed?"

Fenn shrugged, then looked down at his legs and saw he was under a thick, white blanket, but he was sleepy and couldn't be bothered to reply. But someone being sleepy had never stopped Amber before. She jabbed him in the chest with her nail.

"Wake up!" she snapped. "*Wake up!*"

A shriek jolted Fenn awake from his dream and he sat up quickly. It was the middle of the night. A screech owl was skimming over his head, hunting for frogs and mice between the mossy rocks. He had been lying exactly where he'd fallen asleep the night before, on the stubby outcrop of rocks overlooking Halflin's Sunkyard. Halflin always said owls were bad luck and Fenn's stomach knotted in fear. His

21

hand was on his chest where something sharp was digging in and when he pulled it out, there was the brass clover earring Amber had given him the day before to bring him luck. It must have pierced through his pocket and woken him.

It had brought him luck as she'd hoped; Fenn was already covered in a layer of snow but he hadn't felt cold. *Lulls yer ter death quicker than a mermaid*, Halflin had once warned him about the cold. Fenn scrambled to his feet, shaking miniature stalactites from his fringe.

"Tikki?" he croaked. "Tikki!"

The small mound of snow at his feet began to shake and squeak, before cracking open to reveal his rucksack buried beneath. Fenn gently scuffed off the snow and peered inside.

"Tikki?" he called anxiously. There was a mewing as the little mongoose made his way to the opening. He popped his head out of the bag, twitching his whiskers and blinking sleepily at Fenn.

"You shouldn't be in there. It's dangerous," Fenn said, lifting Tikki away from the kerosene-filled bottle-bomb he'd wedged in the corner with Halflin's old leather gauntlets. He'd made four to destroy the Punchlock and this was his last one; it was the only weapon he had.

He rumpled Tikki's fur, making him purr with happiness. As Tikki's warmth seeped into his frost-blistered fingertips, Fenn looked over at the Punchlock. Setting it alight had been the signal to the Resistance that the Demaris had returned; returned to fight the Terra Firma.

Even now it was still burning; the embers of the tarry post shimmered and smouldered, casting a molten orange glow over the tranquil waters of the Sunkyard. Every so often there were sharp spitting sounds, like eggs being cracked into a skillet of hot bacon fat, and suddenly the memory of his last morning with Halflin tried to shoulder its way into Fenn's thoughts. But Fenn was properly awake now and refused it entry, jamming the door closed to his past. That was gone and his beloved grandfather was dead. He had to forget memories like that; it would do no good to remember them. They would bring him pain and make him weak.

The only thing he needed to think about now was the Resistance – and revenge. Chilstone had killed his parents and grandfather, stolen the Sargassons' children and imprisoned thousands of innocent Seaborns, including his old friend Milk. The memory of Milk's pale eyes, blinking in confused terror the night Chilstone's men had made a Sweep on the Shanties, had scarred Fenn's heart. The Resistance needed Fenn as much as he needed them. That's why he'd taken such a risk lighting the Punchlock; it could just as easily bring Chilstone to his door.

He stretched stiffly and scanned the marsh. Thick clouds

bulged over the full moon, making it hard to see much more than the snow-whitened tips of bulrushes. Apart from the odd rasping bark of a marsh fox in the distance, it was quiet as a grave. East Isle's Wall was invisible, yet when Fenn turned in its direction he felt he could see it still. He peered into the marsh's swirling mists, willing there to be a sign of movement, but he knew the truth. The Punchlock had been burning for hours; if anyone was coming, they would have come by now.

There was no Resistance. He was on his own.

When he'd thrown the first bomb, Fenn's heart had been full of fire too. Now it sunk like lead. He gazed bleakly at the smouldering timber, his fingers still throbbing as they returned to life. He felt stupid and alone, wondering what he should do. If the Resistance was dead, he'd have to find others to fight with him. Magpie's words returned to him in a flash, *Sargassons the only ones puttin' up a fight.*

Every Seaborn had reason to fear Chilstone; anyone without the right to live on land was a second-class citizen in the Terra Firma's eyes, but the East Marsh Sargassons didn't just fear Chilstone, they hated him too. It was thirteen years since Chilstone had snatched every child under two years old in his insane hunt for Tomas and Maya's baby. Fenn knew that wounds that deep took more than time to heal. Fenn didn't know where their settlement was, but he'd scour the marsh until he found them, or they found him. They had to have enough fight and anger to match his own.

If he was going to be out on the marsh for weeks he'd need shelter and a weapon to protect him. He had matches, a few candles, his penknife, a sou'wester and shirt, but he'd need something for shelter and ideally a bigger knife. He remembered the sailcloth drying behind the hut and the sharp billhook Halflin used to split kindling. He lifted Tikki up around his neck and carefully put the firebomb upright in his rucksack, wedging it with the shirt he'd taken from the *Ionia* the night they'd buried Lundy, Halflin's old friend who had helped them so much. Then he slipped the rucksack straps over his shoulders and scrambled back down the path towards the hut.

It was so dark he crashed into the wall flanking the back garden, slicing open his knee on the sharp flint, but he was in too much of a hurry to feel the pain. As he approached the hut, the clouds parted enough to let the moonshine through and he saw the ghostly white rectangle of the sailcloth, its coating of white frost glinting in the moonlight. He yanked it off the rope and bundled it into a tight roll, using the rope to tie it to his rucksack. He ran to the cart-shed and tugged the billhook out of the block, wrapped the shirt around the blade and stuffed it deep in the rucksack. Then he slipped back into the hut. The door was ajar, letting a slice of silvery light fall across the floor like a knife. Tikki could smell rats and scampered down Fenn's body to see what he could catch.

First Fenn checked the crate where Halflin stored the rice and grain the Gleaners traded for bacon and rabbit, just in case he'd missed anything the day before. What the Terras hadn't bothered to loot had been spoilt by wild animals. He found a tin and peered inside, but all that was left were husks of millet scattered with mouse droppings. He had just whistled to Tikki to go, when he remembered the old telescope he once used to search out Fearzeros. It'd be useful out on the marsh, and it had been Halflin's when he'd been at sea; he wanted it for that reason alone. As he clambered up the ladder, Tikki scampered up after him and immediately slid off to investigate the crevices beneath the roof, squeaking excitedly.

It was as black as prunes beneath the tiles, too dark to see anything, but Fenn had hidden up there enough times to know every knot and splinter in the wooden boards. Feeling the rough wood like Braille, he inched over to the lookout platform where he'd seen the *Warspite* that fateful morning. He tentatively groped in the dark for the telescope, but instead his fingertips snagged on the jagged edge of metal where the telescope had been wrenched off its stand. The Terras had taken it.

The platform was made from a pallet with a couple of

mothy blankets over it. Anything would be useful to Fenn on his trek. As he bundled one into his rucksack, he heard a tinny clatter in the pitch black.

Fenn felt around again and his fingers alighted on something else: the stub of a candle melted down in a jar. He struck one of the matches he'd taken from the *Salamander* and lit the wick. On the floor nearby was the tin of oats Halflin left there.

Could save yer life if yer stuck up here, Halflin had said as he'd stuffed the tin beneath the pallet. *Take 'em wiv a spit o' water ter puff 'em up an' fill yer.* He'd never forgotten the old tricks he'd learnt aboard the Labour-Ship when the Terras imprisoned him for forgery. Fenn quickly unscrewed the lid to check they were still edible.

He saw it immediately; a triangle of paper poking out of the floury grains, like the sail of a ship. Fenn tugged it out.

The paper was thin and folded many times to strengthen it into a hard packet, so he had to shake out the oats caught inside. It crackled as he opened it, sparky with its old secret. Inside the first fold was written:

Fenn

He'd never seen his name written before and it was a shock. It was like the first time he'd ever seen his own reflection and noticed his eyes were different colours and weren't the same muddy hazel-brown as Halflin's. He was surprised at two Ns; he'd thought Fenn was spelt with one. Then he began to notice the detail of each letter – the spidery, wobbly line, a splash of ink running from the E. He opened the second fold and read:

If yer in truble get ter the Sargassons

And just beneath this was a single smudged fingerprint: Halflin's. A muscle in Fenn's heart flinched, but he bit back the thought and turned the paper over, spreading it flat on the pallet and smoothing out the creases. He brought the candle closer. It was the first page torn from Fenn's old encyclopaedia.

Chambers's Encyclopaedia of Universal Knowledge
Volume III

Below this were the words "Cadaver to Dragon", although they were barely legible beneath a detailed map. Fenn stared at the precious piece of paper; he needed this knowledge more than tarps or knives. Halflin had drawn all of East Marsh for him, using ink brewed from bark.

The map had which landmarks to watch out for: the

remains of a church tower and a windmill. It showed shipwrecks to shelter in, the few bridges the Terras hadn't destroyed and where the water was shallow enough to wade. On the eastern side of the map, Halflin had drawn the thick bank of Sargassum that had lured the eels to East Isle's marshes, followed by the Sargassons who fished for them. It showed dangers too: the swathe of mudflats across the midsection of the map were dotted to show quicksand, and along the southern coast were the Hellhulks – ancient Fearzeros now turned into prison ships. The main Terra Firma sentry points along East Isle's Wall were also marked out.

Most important of all, Halflin had drawn the old forest. It was forty miles long, stretching from one side of the marsh to the other, and was ten miles deep. It had been planted as a flood defence years before, when the trees had been grown to slow the coming tsunamis. It had nearly worked, but the last Rising was so huge it had swept over the forest, engulfing it and turning the fresh water salty. Most of the trees had died. Now twisting around the dying or petrified trees were tangles of rivers and creeks to lead a mapless traveller lost beyond finding. Apart from Sargassons who fished for eels there and Seaborn strays whose boats were marooned, Halflin always told Fenn the forest was uninhabitable, perhaps to stem his curiosity. But in the

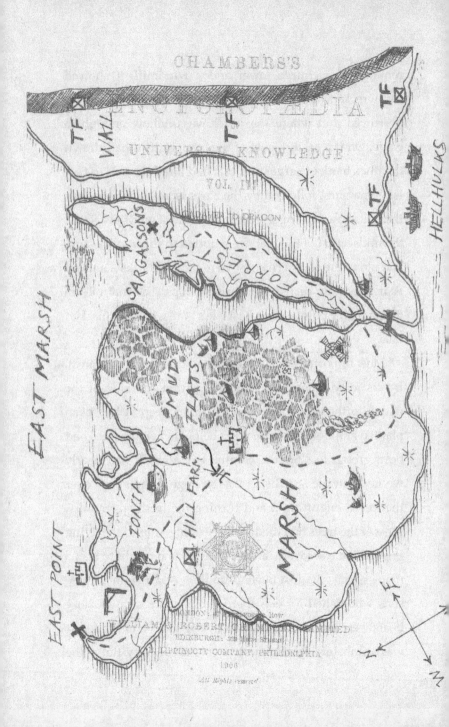

uppermost corner of the forest, was a scratched cross next to the word "Sargassons". The Sargasson settlement was a closely guarded secret, but Halflin had lived and worked on the marsh all his life and knew it like the back of his hand. He had mapped the Sargasson territory so Fenn could find their settlement too. With the last Demari to rally them, Fenn was sure they could defeat Chilstone and the Terra Firma once and for all. He stared at the map a few moments longer to commit it to memory before carefully buttoning it in his pocket.

He had everything there was to take. It was time to go. There wasn't much of the night left and he wanted to travel as far as he could before daylight. He took one last look around the gloomy loft and was about to blow out the candle when he spied a chink of light through one of the loosened tiles. His heart quickening with excitement, he crouched down and peered through the tiles. Dozens of lights freckled the marshes, moving quickly towards the burning Punchlock. Fenn couldn't believe it; the Resistance had come after all!

"Tikki!" Fenn called, light-headed with excitement, running back towards the hatch. Tikki bounded up, but just as he sprang up on Fenn's shoulder, Fenn was struck by Halflin's voice again. *Look before yer leap.* He stepped back and looked out through the roof tiles again, straining to make out the approaching figures. He could see the lights flashing from the lanterns but there was something else glinting too; some kind of metal.

The steel truncheons of Terras.

3

Instantly the heat of excitement chilled, like a fever sweat on the skin. There was nowhere for Fenn to run, nowhere to hide. He was trapped. The doors weren't bolted and he didn't have time to get down and out of the back door. Even if he could, he wasn't certain they hadn't surrounded the hut already.

Fenn's heart somersaulted in fear. He blew out the candle flame and gently lowered the trapdoor back into place, softly sliding the bolt to with the heel of his boot, before peeping back through the lookout. Against the Punchlock's glow he could just make out the silhouettes of a group of Terras who had turned a fire-hose on its dying embers. Slurries of wet smoke and steam smeared the lightening sky. Another unit of Terras was running up the path that led from the Punchlock, keeping in the deep shadows cast by the clumps of gorse. Others were already behind the wall encircling the hut. The clouds scudded across the moon again.

Under the cover of this, several of the Terras ran bent-backed towards the hut as if they expected to be shot at. Fenn had a split second to make up his mind.

If not down, then up, he thought. The side of the roof that took the hardest battering from winds off the estuary had been laid with slate tiles. On the other side it had been covered with whatever could be found: reeds woven between branches of elder and squares of purple-black clods cut from the marsh. It had needed replacing a year before, but now Fenn was glad the winter had been too cold for Halflin to get on with the job. It should be rotten enough for him to push his way out.

Fenn put his palms flat under the reeds above his head and gave it a hard shove, making a hole large enough to climb through. Just as he was about to clamber out, he heard a thumping from the room below and the sound of someone coming up the ladder.

"Someone's up there!"

Tikki squeaked in fear at the sound of the Terras' shouts. The hatch shook as one of the Terras heaved his shoulder against it.

"Give yourself up. You've got nowhere to go!"

The hatch bounced again. Fenn ripped open his rucksack

and lifted out the last firebomb as Tikki hopped back in.

Fenn carefully propped the firebomb next to the hatch. He lit the wick and scrambled out onto the roof. As soon as he'd squeezed through the hole, he heard the hatch crash open, but he didn't look back. He was already skidding down the reeds towards the pigsty. His heart seemed to slow with thickening blood as adrenalin surged through his veins. *Run, keep on running,* came Halflin's voice in his head. Fenn landed on the pigsty roof and rolled across the black slates, jagged as crow's wings.

The second after he landed, the bomb went off, followed by a loud crash as part of the hut's roof was blasted into the air. The force of the explosion knocked Fenn off the pigsty. Sky, slate and flame twisted in a sickening spiral as he crashed with a smack on the frosty ground. Pain snapped like teeth around his lungs, making everything sharp and clear again.

A spurt of orange flame shot out through a hole in the thatch. From inside, Fenn heard the shouts and screams of the terrified Terras.

Geddup! came the voice in his head.

Fenn lurched to his feet, his eyes watering as he tried to grab a breath in vain. As he staggered away he took a quick look over his shoulder, just in time to see three Terras bolting from the hut, flames licking down their clothing and over their masks. They plunged into the pigs' water troughs and rolled over in the snow to douse the fire as other Terras ran up to help. Fenn skidded around the pigsties to get out of view and threw himself down on the ground. He wrenched open the rucksack to check Tikki hadn't been hurt when they fell. In the corner of the rucksack a tiny ball of fur was bunched up, shivering.

"Good boy!" Fenn whispered. There wasn't time for more. He slapped back the rucksack flap and stumbled head-first into the dark.

A white crust of snow on the old oak tree soon gave Fenn his bearings and he careened towards it, diving around the other side, gasping for air as he pressed his back up against the trunk, the hard knobbles of warty bark pushing through his coat. He listened out for the sound of Terras but still no one was following.

He gulped in breath in shuddering spasms as he tried to remember which way he was supposed to go. It was so dark it was pointless getting the map out again and he didn't have time anyway. Instead he pictured it in his mind's eye: the path led past the Ionia and on towards an old shipwreck on the edge of the mudflats.

He tightened the rucksack's strap across his waist to keep it from getting yanked off as he passed through the gorse. He wrapped his scarf tight against his face to protect it, then plunged into the reed beds.

He ran non-stop for the next two hours, until morning burst onto the marsh. Halflin could recognise the signs of solid ground better than Fenn: one moment he was on it, the next, he was waist-deep in slimy water, clawing at reeds to pull himself out. He couldn't find the passage Halflin had followed – an avenue hollowed out by muntjac and foxes. Instead, Fenn kept going even though the reeds split open his skin like razor blades. The first cut stung cruelly, but after that he ceased to notice; all he worried about was if Tikki was getting bruised or if he was scared.

Fenn darted left and right in zigzags to hide the course he was cutting through the reed beds. He wouldn't cover quite so much ground this way, but he'd be harder to follow. He went on like this, until the fiery orange sun was over the horizon and the birds from all over the marsh had woken. Curlews and lapwings began whistling, their chorus swelling as the sun rose higher.

Fenn ran through the pain of a searing stitch until suddenly, from the corner of his eye, he caught a flash of fiery red in the distance through the reeds. He stopped; far off he could see the *Ionia*'s windows, reflecting the golden light. The sight filled him with hope and he congratulated himself on his sense of direction – not bad for his first time out in the marsh alone.

Triumphantly he ran up the snow-speckled track that ran along the tributary the *Panimengro* had come into. Here, reeds gave way to clumps of furze, which provided hardly any cover. Fenn was trotting so close to the furze that he only just avoided blinding himself on a branch sticking out into his path; he dodged, snagged his foot on something and fell sprawling onto the ground. A thin, almost invisible piece of wire, glinting like spider thread, lay across the short mossy grass. He tugged the wire from the gorse; at its end was a rabbit, freshly dead, its body still limp and warm. One of Lundy's snares. Fenn stuffed the rabbit in his pocket and unhooked the wire from the peg in the ground; a snare like that would be useful. He was just about to head on when he sensed something was wrong. It was quiet; too quiet. The rest of the marsh was full of birdsong, but here it was silent.

He inched closer through the reeds until he was near enough to see the sward of land banked up by the Ionia. Thrushes and reed warblers should have been about, pulling fresh worms from the mossy turf as the early sun melted the snow, but no birds were on it this morning. Fenn peered at the ground. A few feet ahead, a stone had been knocked from the earth. He could clearly see the mould of the stone in the soft, damp soil from where it had been dislodged. The cobble was large – at least as big as his own fist, too hefty to have been knocked out by a muntjac, and a wolf would not tread so carelessly. The underside of the stone was still stained with damp; someone had passed here within the last hour. He peered more closely; the moss was thick and velvety, and the morning dew had covered the tiny fronds with millions of minute droplets that glittered white as diamonds.

Fenn laid his cheek on the earth – an old trick Halflin had taught him for when you wanted to find a dropped object too small for the eye to see. There, in the sparkling white dew, was a bright green patch of emerald. A footprint. It wasn't made by the flat deerskin boots of the Sargassons, but had hard ridges on it. A serrated imprint clearly patterned the moss. It was a soldier's boot; a Terra's boot.

They'd been ahead of him all along.

4

Fenn had nearly made a fatal mistake. He'd underestimated his enemy and overestimated himself. He slowly crawled backwards into the reeds, taking care not to stir them.

He slunk away, keeping as low as he could and waded down into the river, holding his rucksack carefully over his head. Once he was a good distance from the *Ionia*, he climbed back up to high land and ran back along the edge of the tributary, following it into the marsh.

Fenn ran blindly, completely forgetting the landmarks he was supposed to aim for in the huge expanse of marsh, only telling himself he'd stop at the next clump of bramble, the next burst of gorse flower. At last cramp caught him, stabbing pains shooting up through his legs. Once it had subsided he looked up and realised he was in a sparse patch of bulrushes, growing by a wide, oily bank where the tributary shallowed out into a muddy beach. He was lost. Blood thunderclapped in Fenn's head, as if he was going to faint. He put his hands on his knees and lowered his head like Halflin had once told him, to cure dizziness. Through his knees, upside down, he saw a copse of scraggy alder trees growing up through the ribs of a wrecked boat on the far bank. It had probably been washed up in one of the Risings. Thousands of empty ships still floated on the oceans, unsinkable yet unsailable; their hulls strong enough to stay afloat, but their masts and rudders ripped off in storms. He stood up and lowered the rucksack to the ground and gently lifted Tikki out. Tikki stood up on his hind legs, wrinkling his nose at the briny scent of dank kelp before sneezing so hard he knocked himself over backwards. Fenn burst out laughing, making Tikki squeak with angry embarrassment before giving himself a quick preen to show he didn't care, and scurrying off to explore.

While Tikki chased bulrush seeds drifting on the salty breeze, Fenn studied the map, but it didn't tally with what he could see. Beyond this wreck there was supposed to be a church tower still standing on the edge of mudflats. Halflin had warned him not to cross the flats – they were too dangerous without the right equipment. He had drawn Fenn's path accordingly, taking his route down and around the mudflats, then up again towards the Sargassons' forest; a journey that could take him several days. But Fenn reckoned he might save himself a day's walk if he tried. He also knew he needed to rest soon, or he'd make a stupid mistake and run headlong into the Terras again. But he couldn't stop in the open like this. He'd get across to the old boat and hide; at least he'd have a decent view over the marsh. Perhaps he could even spend the night there.

He folded away the map and stepped down onto the shore, but stopped just in time, teetering on the brink of another step. The mud was patterned with a mosaic of dozens of prints, mainly those of birds. A lone snipe had crossed paths with a heron and one had dropped a crab, before both took flight, shown by the scatter of wet grit on the mud's surface. A few feet away, the crab was lying on its back, courageously pinching the air with its remaining claw, unaware that its enemies had fled; fled because they had caught sight of a lone wolf slinking through the thin crop of bulrushes. The wolf's prints were light and closely paced as it stalked its prey, but its returning prints showed it had dragged something large, scuffing a track through the bubbling green algae that coated the bank. It was easier for Fenn to read what had happened on the mudflat, than read one sentence in the encyclopaedia.

If he walked across it, he would never be able to hide his

tracks, but as the Terras already knew he was on the marsh, hiding wasn't enough. He scraped over the footprints he'd already left and took a long stride over to a small drift of shingle that ran between the rushes. Now Tikki had finished off the dying crab, Fenn clucked to him and he ran up onto his shoulders, curling affectionately around his neck. Fenn walked backwards down the bank to the boat, taking care to make his footprints clearly visible; making sure that any Terra Firma seeing it would think he'd walked upriver away from the wrecked boat, instead of down towards it.

As he reached the boat, he realised it was an old wooden Seiner, and must have been there for at least thirty years, because the alder trees growing right through it were already twice Fenn's height. It looked as if it had nosedived into the marsh – as it could have, if a wave had been forceful enough to thrust it there. Or it may have been wrecked out at sea, its crew drowned, then the empty ship was perhaps caught on a rogue wave and brought up the tributary to rest here in the river's kink. Fenn had watched such waves sometimes rip up through the creeks around the Sunkyard. They were powerful enough to tip a boat to its gunwales if the crew didn't know what they were doing. The Seiner's stern was clear of the mud, and sea snails clustered in its shadow like tiny cobblestones. Tikki immediately jumped down and scrabbled amongst them, knocking the empty snail shells around as if he was playing a game of marbles.

Halflin had told Fenn that hundreds of such wrecks dotted the marsh. They'd sometimes appear overnight, after a storm, and the Sargassons would strip the wood away, like crows picking carrion clean to the bone, until all that was left were a few ribs, or a mast, then – the next morning – nothing. Fenn was surprised to see a wooden boat left untouched like this. A waste; there was firewood for a half-winter at least.

He jammed his knife into the side of the boat, wedged his foot in a porthole, and levered himself up. On seeing Fenn's feet disappear over the edge of the boat, Tikki let out a whimper and snatched the biggest snail, before jumping up by Fenn's side.

On deck, the gunwales had been rubbed to nothing by the wet winds slicing off the marsh, and only a few joists were left sticking up around the sides of the deck, bleached to the colour of bones. A wet slick of lichen and browning moss coated the rotting planks, and Fenn could see a dank cabin below. Alders, with rosy catkins flushing their branches, thrust up between the wood and speckling the deck were dozens of tiny cones. Delighted by new toys to play with, Tikki dropped the snail disdainfully, nudged it towards Fenn and ran off down the deck, making the cones bounce and scatter, chasing his own tail in excitement.

Fenn gingerly edged over to the hatch and looked in; the ladder was still sound and he climbed down – it'd be good to hide in while he rested. It was so cold it hurt Fenn's lungs and his breath hung in the damp cabin before dissolving. Spokes of light stabbed in from the deck above, and he could still hear the patter of Tikki's claws as he raced around above him. It took him a few moments before his eyes grew accustomed to the darkness, and when they did he realised there was a sheet of rusted corrugated iron leaning against the side of the hull and a ring of cobbles encircling some soot-blackened boards. Someone was living here.

Just at that moment Tikki skittered down, chattering wildly as he jumped onto Fenn's back. Fenn tried to grab him but missed, twisting as he fell and knocking over the rusting iron. As it disintegrated into flaky shards, Fenn's eyes fell on a few bones scattered on the ground behind it. He knelt down to take a look, nudging one with a stick. There was also a blanket covering something. Fenn tentatively lifted it away with the tip of the stick before jolting back. It was a skull.

Fenn scrabbled backwards to the other side of the cabin, as far away as possible, his back pressed to the crumbling wood of the Seiner's hull. Tikki immediately ran back to him, licking his face to make Fenn feel better. The skull must have been lying there for a very long time. Probably a

Seaborn on the run; maybe just lost on the marsh after one of the Risings. The Great Rising had seen the highest number drowned, but there had been many tidal surges since. There was nothing to say how the person died; nothing left except bones, disturbed only by the tide that still sluiced through the bottom of the boat's hull, widening the rotten gaps in its sides. Fenn understood why the boat had been left to rot now. No Sargasson would ever rob a grave. He grabbed Tikki tightly and hurried back up the ladder onto the deck.

Still shuddering with fright, he clambered onto the gunwale, scanning the horizon to see if he could find the church tower Halflin had drawn. Winds flattened the reeds to a rolling sea of green, but in the distance he saw a small, low speck sticking out through the green swathes. He checked the map again, jumped down from the Seiner and set off.

By the time he reached the church tower, the icy creeks the sun had melted were now freezing over again and he was chilled to the bone. Only twenty feet of the tower still remained above ground. It was ancient; the walls were made of polished flint, encrusted with mottled lichens. On the corner of each wall, four ugly stone faces, with copper pipes sticking from their mouths, still leered over a village now far beneath the marsh. Someone had boarded up the windows to protect them from the ever-rising waters – but to no avail.

Fenn pushed his way through one of the gaps and looked down into the guts of the tower where oil-black marsh water was climbing the stone steps. He twisted around to look up. The roof had long decayed so he could see the sky, but a few feet above his head the huge old bell still hung from an oak beam, its clapper rusted stiff and silent.

Fenn lowered himself down and opened up the map again to get his bearings, looking out over the flats to find the other wrecks Halflin had marked. Cupping his hands around his eyes he could see one in the distance, sticking up starkly on the horizon. He frowned as he tried to gauge how long it would take him to reach it. Silvery mud, stretched on for miles, with no cover save for the scraggy clumps of glasswort and waxy tufts of purslane. He would be easily visible on such flat ground, unless he could think of a way to disguise himself. He remembered Lundy's cloak of burweed and rushes.

Around the tower grew flushes of water horsetail, speckled with its first buds. Fenn gathered an armful and some whippy stems of broom. Leaning against the tower and letting the sun-warmed stones heat his back, he set to work. He pulled the blanket out and cut the edges to make a tie. Then he made small nicks where a cape would cross his shoulders and wove a few strands of broom in between, then laced horsetail through until he'd covered the blanket completely.

When he'd finished, he laid the cape on the ground to assess his work. It wasn't as good as Lundy's, but it'd do.

He needed to get to the wreck before dark. In daylight, he stood half a chance of seeing where the quicksand was, but after dark he'd be done for. He walked a few, experimental steps out, just to see how wet the sands were. Within seconds his feet were being sucked in deep; it would be twice the effort to walk across if his every step was dragged down. From his viewing platform at the hut, Fenn had often spied on the Sargassons bringing their catch back from the creeks on sledges pulled by horses. To stop the horses being sucked into the mud, they fitted them with mud boots; wide pieces of wood to spread their weight. He needed something similar.

Searching around, his eyes alighted on the loose planks over the windows. He prised them off and laid the wood flat on the ground, spiking his knife in to grind holes a few inches apart. Using strips torn from the sailcloth, he made webbing to strap them to his feet.

Fenn picked up a few heavy stones that had fallen from the church tower and threw the grass cape over his shoulders. Then he stepped out onto the glistening mud. He didn't sink, but nor could he move quickly. It was impossible to lift his feet high, so instead he perfected a type of skating shuffle, skimming over the wet mudflats. Each time he saw a patch of darker-coloured mud he took out one of the stones and threw it down. If it sank immediately, he knew there was quicksand and he'd slowly edge around it. If the stone remained visible, he knew he was safe. At his approach, egrets flapped up from tugging lugworms from the sand and splintered into the sky like shards of flint.

The sea wind shivered the sands and the air dampened. Then the rain came, at first light, then so hard the mud jumped and spat, making a bank of deepening murk all around him. Fenn thought about turning back; he could at least shelter against the church tower, sleeping under the sailcloth. But there was a wet bank of mist between him and the shoreline and he wasn't sure which way to go. He stopped and looked around, blinking as the water streamed off his cape and into his eyes and ears.

Then he heard it. He pushed his scarf away from his ears and listened hard: a high-pitched whirr drifted over the marsh, accompanied by a thrashing sound like a giant propeller. Something was driving towards him like an enormous carving knife, slicing through the reed beds. It was a Swampscrew. The Terras had finally caught up with him.

5

Fenn flung himself down and spread his arms like a bat's wings to make himself flatter. He'd never seen a Swampscrew before but Halflin had described them to him. He slowly turned his head to see how close it was. A cloud of silt was being thrown high into the air obscuring it; then suddenly it was in view, whirring and clanking, reducing the church tower to rubble, spitting stone in the air. The noise was deafening.

The main body of the vehicle was made of polished steel and it was open-topped like a raft, with a rail enclosing the battalion of Terras it carried. At the front of the deck was a cabin and the rest of the deck was taken up by three fuel tanks. Its sides comprised huge steel plates, overlapping each other like the scales of an armadillo. Two giant cylinders, sharp as ploughshares turned like huge screws and left deep black scars in their wake as the Swampscrew was propelled forwards.

The Swampscrew sliced down the bank towards the flats, leaving a huge spiral of peat behind it, like an enormous potato peeling. It churned relentlessly towards the spot where Fenn lay trembling on the ground, frozen in fear. The noise of ripped earth tore through his head and his teeth juddered with the vibrations. The Swampscrew was moving slowly but steadily; a hundred feet away, then eighty, now sixty. Fenn squeezed his eyes tight shut, clenching his teeth as the Swampscrew trundled on. If he moved they'd spot him immediately; if he didn't move he'd be killed.

Just as he could smell the fumes and the first sprays of mud spattered his cape, he heard a yell. The Swampscrew's engine wound down and the huge cylinders spun to a standstill. Fenn took a gasp of air, terrified. They must have seen him.

"We camp here!" the captain hollered. "Light's going. Could be out on this bog here for all we know. Don't want to go miss him."

He signalled to the driver to cut the engine and hopped up onto the Swampscrew's bow rail. He took out a telescope, sweeping over the flats while his men pegged a tarpaulin over the deck for the night's shelter from the rain.

For a brief moment Fenn couldn't believe his luck. Forty

feet more and he would have been crushed. But then it sunk in: he was too close to the Terras to slip away in daylight – he'd be spotted immediately. And moving after dark risked being sucked into the quicksand; a slow and frightening death. If any of the Terras looked hard in his direction, there was every chance they would see him; the tufts of purslane weren't enough to cover the unnatural mound he made on the mudflats. Tikki chattered under the cloak; he could smell Fenn's fright and balled up against him, whimpering. Fenn slowly shifted him to the warmth and dark of his jacket, hoping it might calm him. He pressed his cheek against the wet ground and cocked his ear to hear any snatches of their conversation that might give him a clue of what they planned to do.

"The kid's a tricky one," he heard one of the Terras grumble.

The captain jumped down from the deck next to the one who'd spoken, glaring hard at him. "That stunt at the Sunkyard may have caught us off guard, but there are two more of these beasts on the marsh." He slapped the Swampscrew's panels, like a rider satisfied with his mount. "Remember, he's just a kid like all the others. Nothing we haven't seen before – just another marsh rat. He'll be lying low, probably in a wreck. Maybe even *that* one," he continued as he pointed across the gleaming silver mud to the very wreck Fenn had been on his way to.

"Can't check them all!" one of the men complained, but the captain cuffed him on the head as he passed by. "That's *exactly* what we do, then we burn them to the ground. The kid knows the marsh, but we've got the equipment," he said. "We're systematic. Organised. An army, not a straggle of Seaborns."

"Nothin' beats Malmuts though. They're what we need," one of the men muttered.

The captain turned sharply. "A shipment's due tomorrow morning. You!" he bellowed, singling out the one who had spoken up. "Keep watch first." He gestured to the Swampscrew. "Rest of you, clean her up!"

The Terra crew knew better than to argue that it was pointless to clean a Swampscrew while they were still out in the muddy marsh. They began wetting rags to shine up the armoured plates. Meanwhile, the captain strolled idly around the machine, checking the rail, testing the blades of the cylinders for their sharpness. Then he climbed aboard again and disappeared under the tarpaulin on deck.

The rain pattered on the woven branches of Fenn's cape, the way it used to tap on the slate roof of the pigsty. He kept still for what seemed to be hours, until he thought the men had probably settled for the night. Then he edged his body around in the wet mud like the slow hand of a clock until he could see the night watchmen properly.

Shivering beneath his cape, his teeth chattering uncontrollably, Fenn listened as the first watchers moaned about the marsh, the Sargassons and the weather and cursed the damp wood as their tiny fire dwindled. They were so close he could smell the smoke and hear every word. As he listened his mind raced through his options: he wouldn't stand a chance once the Malmuts arrived, but he'd sooner die trying to escape than disappear down a sinkhole of sand. He would wait until dawn when hopefully the Terras would be asleep, then he'd try to crawl away. He wouldn't have much of a head start on the dogs, but it was the only chance he had.

Darkness fell quickly on the flats and the air turned icy. As the long hours passed, the night winds picked up, battering the Swampscrew's tarpaulin like a sail. The watch changed but the Terras stayed alert, terrified of Sargasson raids and wild creatures. The darkness also brought other noises that Fenn understood but the Terras only feared: murderous barks of marsh foxes and the lonely howls of wolves. The rushes in Fenn's cape had hardened into an icy yoke across his neck. Hearing the wolves, Tikki crawled down even further from where Fenn had pushed him into safety. He must have been hungry yet he didn't go off hunting; instead he lay quiet and trembling under the crook of

Fenn's arm. It was as if Tikki understood the danger and the need for absolute still. Fenn managed to bend his arm back around so he could just reach Tikki. He stroked Tikki's chest with his thumb, smoothing the dense fur down and rippling it back again, and murmured quietly reassuring sounds. Fenn was more afraid than ever, but he concentrated all his thoughts into the little patch of warmth under Tikki's head. At last he heard Tikki begin to purr contentedly and fall asleep.

The night tides rolled up the flats, sloshing over the banks of bladderwrack. Fenn was high enough on the sandbank to keep mainly dry, but even so the returning water swept up and down, washing over his feet. Once he thought he could hear something shifting in the sands, but the sludge of snow clouds still made it too dark to see what it was.

As night stretched on, Fenn's thoughts began to drift to what would happen if they captured him. They would want to find out who had helped him. They would hurt him. He knew he wasn't strong like Halflin. He'd be in pain, he'd be afraid, he'd tell Chilstone anything to make pain stop. He held Tikki tighter, wondering if he should try to get him to run away to safety right now; wondering if he'd even go.

To divert himself, Fenn turned his thoughts to his friends. They'd be well under way to West Isle by now. He hoped they'd get beyond its Wall. He remembered being on the *Salamander* that night, how they'd talked about ways to survive the floods. He closed his eyes and let his memory drift across the *Salamander*'s deck, watching the brazier twinkle and almost smelling the wonderful chocolate drink Comfort made. He thought of Gulper, Amber, Fathom and poor Milk, the only friends he'd ever had, apart from Tikki. For the first time since he'd waved them goodbye, Fenn let himself think of how much he missed them all. If this was to be his last night alive, he'd spend it with his friends – even if it was only in his imagination. Lost in these thoughts he drifted into an uneasy sleep.

Fenn had been dreaming of Amber's tin mug jangling as she toasted to a better life, then the clatter became real. He realised with a jolt that he'd slept too long. The clanking sounds came from the Terra camp; the night watchman was hammering a spoon against a can for the wake-up call.

Dawn had passed and Fenn was too late to escape unseen. In the night he had ground his head into a hollow of sand to try and flatten himself out as much as possible to avoid detection, so now he couldn't see anything except a clump of slimy bladderwrack seaweed close to his face. He sniffed and a rank smell seeped into his nostrils. The tide was going out now but was making a soft *slup-slup-slup* as if it was lapping against something.

Fenn slowly turned his head to look towards the Terras' camp, making the tiniest movements so that if one of the Terras glanced his way, they might think it was just the ebb of the tide. Peering into the greying light, Fenn looked for the Swampscrew and the tents.

But it was as if it had all disappeared under a gigantic, mouldering hill. Fenn squeezed his eyes shut, then opened them again in case he was still dreaming. He wasn't. Less than ten feet away, washed up on a ridge of mud, lay a huge whale completely blocking his sightline of the Terras – and theirs of him.

The whale was lying twisted, its head rolled to one side so that Fenn could see the lips of its blowhole. It must have been dead for days, because the flesh was starting to sag and tear, and rips had appeared in its sides. Fenn could see one long, red-mottled rib, like a giant tooth sticking out and dozens of suction-cup scars showed that it had battled giant squids. A gaping hole revealed where the poor creature's liver had been torn out, and Fenn remembered Halflin saying that gangs of Orcas would single out a sperm whale. Her beautiful mussel-black tail had been robbed of an entire fluke and there were serrated edges where sharks had taken bites as she drifted past. Hundreds of little holes pocked her skin like moth-nibbles in wool, where other scavengers had fed. The ocean, like land, is a great loop of life with links of death and birth. As Fenn stared, he heard shouts from behind it: cries of disgust as the Terras were woken by the stench.

Stiff as a board, Fenn crawled over the mud to the right, to see how close the Terras were. Tikki squeaked and shifted under the flap of his coat. The captain was settled on the ledge of the Swampscrew, foaming his face for a shave while he angled the wing mirror to see. Most of the crew set about taking down the tents but several were on the ground, laughing and jostling each other towards the rotten whale, scarves wound around their faces as they lobbed stones at its bloated side, trying to puncture it. Fenn pressed himself deeper into the mud. It only needed one of them to come closer on a sightseeing tour of the whale to spot him, but luckily for Fenn, the captain was in a hurry to get going.

"Strike camp!" he yelled, flipping open his razor and quickly scraping soap off his face. The men jumped into action and the sergeant flattened a map on the Swamp-screw's windshield for the captain to see.

"Two more wrecks here and here, sir," he said, jabbing a finger at two points on the map. The captain glanced over, grunting in annoyance as he cut himself. He flicked the pink-tinted foam from his razor and wiped the blade clean on his thigh. The sergeant handed him a towel.

"The other battalions have those areas covered," the captain muttered. "Our mission extends to the Sargasson borders. We can't get the Swampscrew across the bigger rivers without the floating bridges anyway. They arrive in a few days. Until then we don't enter their territory." He laughed and clapped the sergeant's shoulder. "Remember, one fight at a time; we'll fight the Bog-men another day."

He mopped his bleeding cheek with the towel before tossing it at a young Terra nearby. "You! Got good eyesight?" he asked. Months at sea and a poor diet had wrecked the captain's own vision, although he wasn't much above twenty. The boy nodded uncertainly. "Then you go ahead. We'll take it slow so you can check for quicksands." He jumped back onto the deck and shouted, "Start her up!"

As the Swampscrew shuddered into life, the last Terras jumped back on. The cylinders spun until mud began shooting from them like sleet. The boy chosen to check for quicksands tentatively stepped out onto the flats, poking the mud with a long pole. The Swampscrew slowly scythed down the slope behind him. He raised his hand for the direction the Swampscrew needed to take.

"Bear left!" the captain shouted.

Fenn knew he'd have to move quickly; either the boy would see him or he would be crushed as the Swampscrew ploughed past the whale. He had to take his chance now. While the captain had been talking Fenn had been weighing up his options. He realised he'd been wrong: there was one place to hide from sight. He dragged himself up, wincing at the stiffness that tightened across his body and, clutching Tikki, forced himself to run across the mud – not away from the Terras and the Swampscrew, but towards them and the whale. Within a few paces he was at the whale's side, pressing his body tight against the grey underbelly, blistered with sulphuric-yellow barnacles. He scrambled towards the whale's head, ripped off the cape and pushed his rucksack and mud boards under it. He heard the Swampscrew grinding closer; he had seconds left.

Fenn wound his scarf around his head, covering his whole face, then steadying himself with one hand on the rubbery flesh, he jammed his foot in the crease of the whale's jaw, stuck his knife in to get a purchase on the skin and quickly hauled himself up to the blowhole. He understood enough about whale anatomy to know that it wasn't a hole at all, but actually one, single giant nostril, although it really looked more like a toothless black mouth. The blowhole was nearly two feet long – just wide enough for someone as skinny as Fenn to squeeze inside.

He took in a huge suck of air, packing it deep down in his lungs, then put his arms close to his ears, like he was taking a dive, and pushed in, squeezing his hands, arms, head and shoulders through the rubbery lips. He wriggled and jerked his way down, until he heard a slurp as the lips of the blowhole closed behind him. He was plunged into a red-tinted dark, like when he used to pretend to be asleep but looked through his lids at the kitchen lamp.

The blowhole led in at a slight incline, so at first it felt like he would slip deep into the whale's skull and never get out, but he stuck his knife in further to make sure he didn't slip too far. The wet lining bulged against him like cold jelly but by keeping his head tucked down, he found he could still breathe, taking in short breaths to add to his stored lungful. As soon as he had wriggled in he felt the blubbery skin begin to close around his legs, as if it was sucking him in. He arched his back, so he could bring his knees up into the space, then he opened up the jacket flap a little, expelling a mouthful of air towards Tikki to help him breathe. All he had to do now was sit tight for a few minutes until the Terras were out of range.

But each second felt like an hour as he listened to the Swampscrew slowly edge out further onto the mudflats. He wasn't sure how long he could last. The smell and the lack of oxygen were stifling and it was a battle not to be sick. He braced himself against the pressure of the blubber swelling against him in a sticky mass. Any fractional movement caused blasts of gas and bubbles to gush and pop around him. Even with his mask, it made his eyes stream. He clucked at Tikki to help keep him calm, but he could feel his little heart beating fast with panic at the strange smells around him. At last there came a roaring as the Swampscrew churned past the whale's tail, making everything shudder. A few minutes later, Fenn was left alone in silence.

The stench was unbearable and Fenn couldn't breathe properly any more; the gas was making him so light-headed he was struggling not to pass out. He started trying to wriggle his way out, but he didn't seem able to move; if anything, the suction inside the whale seemed to be pulling him in deeper. He got the strongest sense the whale was starting to absorb him; for the first time in his life he could understand how drowning felt. Tikki whimpered in fear.

Fenn started to panic. He tried to push his hands out to get some kind of grip but it was too slippery. He kicked out but his feet just bounced back. He slid in a little more. It dawned on him that it wasn't that different from falling into quicksand. He immediately stopped moving so roughly and remembered his knife. Using it like a hook, he picked and clawed his way around until he was facing out again, then bit by bit he tugged himself up towards the blowhole. He pushed through the mouth and tumbled out, flopping down exhausted onto the mud.

He wiped the slime from his face and blinked into the distance. Far across the flats he could see mud frothing up from where the Swampscrew was churning towards the old wreck the captain had spotted. He watched as the Terras jumped down and disappeared inside, the Swampscrew still clanking. Fenn pulled Tikki out from his coat, grabbed his rucksack from where it was still hidden under the whale and dropped Tikki inside. Then he scrambled around the other side of the whale where he could put on his cape and mud shoes out of sight. As soon as he was ready to go, he peeped around the edge of the whale's tail – just in time to see flames start to lick up around the old wooden wreck. It had been less than three minutes, but the Terras were already packing away their fire-hoses and boarding the Swampscrew. Tikki poked his head up out of the rucksack, twitching his nose in alarm at the unnatural scent of burning tar on the wind.

"Bet you didn't think being nearly caught by them was a good thing, Tikki?" Fenn whispered. "We could have been in that – still asleep! Some wake-up call that would have been!" Fenn gently pushed Tikki's head back inside and buckled down the rucksack's straps. Tikki would be better off in the peaceful, warm dark.

Then he hoisted it on his back, hurrying away in the opposite direction from the Swampscrew, running up the bulldozed banks of the mudflats back towards the path Halflin had always intended him to take.

6

As soon as Fenn was clear of the mudflats he kicked off the wooden shoes and ran to the remains of the church tower, where he slumped against a heap of rubble, catching his breath. Once he'd recovered, he jumped up and hurtled southwards, keeping parallel to the mudflats. There was no cover save the wind-dried stumps of sedge grass and the odd scrawny tree bent to the winds, but if the Terras caught up with him, he figured he could at least take his chances in the boggy reeds.

He ran until the sun faded behind foggy clouds and he felt dizzy with hunger. He stumbled behind a thin crop of willows by a muddy creek, refilled his flask with its stagnant water and opened the rucksack. Instantly Tikki sprang out like a jack-in-the-box, chattering with anger at his captivity, before skittering into the spit of water, where he rolled himself around to clean off the stench of the dead whale. Fenn would have copied him, but he hoped the sour-milk smell of the wax coating his clothes would mask human scent from the Malmuts. He watched Tikki splash and jump in the water while he emptied the rucksack, searching for the tin of oats. His heart sank as he realised the tin must have fallen out when he'd climbed inside the whale. There was nothing to eat but the rabbit and no way to eat it. He let it flop on the ground, wishing he could build a fire, but knowing it'd be far too dangerous. Instead he scraped up what was left of the oats that had fallen out in the bottom of the bag and was about to stuff them in his mouth, when he felt two beady eyes on him. Fenn sighed.

"OK. You have them. I wasn't that hungry anyway," he said scattering them on the ground. Tikki gobbled them up. "At least you get supper," Fenn laughed, giving Tikki a stroke.

Fenn scouted around to see if there was anything else he might be able to eat, but it was too early for frogs to be out of hibernation and the bulrush heads would give him hardly any nourishment. Then he spotted a few leaves at their base, breaking above the waterline. Water parsnip! Halflin used to pick them to bulk out stews. They would be bitter eaten raw, but it was still food. Hungrily, he dug his hands in the mud until he felt the chunky roots deep in the ground and wrenched them out. He was about to cram them in his mouth when something – some old memory – made him pause. The leaves were the wrong shape; too fern-like. It wasn't water parsnip, it was water hemlock. Fenn dropped the roots like hot coals and plunged his hands in the mud, scraping at his fingers with the head of a bulrush. Even the juice was enough to blister the skin; if he'd eaten them, he'd have been dead in twenty minutes.

He stumbled back up the bank cursing his stupidity. The bulrush heads sneezed white seeds in the air as he brushed by and he stuffed a few cottony handfuls in his mouth, crawling back to the refuge of the willows to eat. Tikki followed him, and started jumping up against one of the trunks and snapping at it.

The bark seemed to be moving. Raft spiders, birch bugs, crickets, water boatmen; all insects that should have been hibernating were clambering up into the tree's slender branches. Fenn watched them, puzzled; it was never a good sign when marsh life broke its own rules. Tikki at last caught something and bounded onto Fenn's shoulder, with two spindly legs sticking out of his mouth. He gifted a half-chewed spider onto Fenn's shoulder for him to eat.

"Very noble of you," Fenn said, "but I'll stick to my tasteless fluff, thanks." He pushed the spider back to Tikki, who didn't hesitate to gobble it down. But as he ruffled

Tikki's fur, there came a faint but unmistakable sound: a Malmut barking.

Instantly Tikki picked up his fear and began to growl. Fenn jumped up trying to think straight; he needed to run, but he was frozen to the spot. He remembered Milk standing terrified in the alleyway during the Shanties Sweep. This must have been what had happened to him. Fenn had been running for so long, scared for so long, that his body rebelled. Sweat broke on his neck and instantly the dogs' barks changed to a keen yelping as they caught his scent. Where were they? Two miles away at least, and yet they could still smell Fenn. They were coming for him.

Think! Fenn told himself. *Think! What would Halflin do?*

Halflin wouldn't panic. He wouldn't fall victim to his own fear. He'd make a plan. No one could outrun a Malmut; instead Fenn would have to slow them, mislead them. His clothes stank of dead whale but he was also sweating with fear – something Malmuts were bred to detect. He'd have to disguise that. He dived down the muddy bank, smearing his face and arms with treacly black mud as he went, wiping it over his neck where his skin was prickling the most. Then he stuffed his hands into Halflin's gauntlets to protect them, grabbed the hemlock roots he'd just chucked and sliced their white flesh into slivers. His hands were trembling as he grabbed the rabbit. If it couldn't be a meal for him, it could be a weapon. Malmuts' sense of smell would be both their strength and their downfall. Honed to hunt frightened humans above all else, the animals lacked other senses; they wouldn't even taste the sickly-sweet hemlock. If the Malmuts weren't suspicious, the Terras wouldn't be either and it only needed a single Malmut to take the bait for the whole battalion to be slowed: a sick dog would have to be carried by the men.

Fenn took a deep breath. In his mind's eye he saw Halflin skin a rabbit so the pelt didn't get bloodstained. He'd make a shallow cut along the rabbit's body and the legs, cutting around the feet, leaving fur as if the rabbit were wearing slippers. Then he'd pull off the rest of the fur, like peeling off a too-tight jumper. The rabbit was suddenly so tiny, naked, no longer a rabbit: a meal, covered in a thin, veiny membrane. He must not pierce that membrane. He mustn't get blood on the rabbit's fur. He mustn't leave any sign it had been tampered with.

Fenn carefully pushed the tip of his knife into the fur and quickly worked his fingers between the fur and membrane, separating the fibrous connection to make a tiny pocket. He pushed some hemlock inside. He made a few more openings all over the rabbit, each no bigger than his little fingernail, and pushed hemlock into each one. Then he laid the rabbit gently on the ground.

"Bring me luck," he whispered and ran.

He ran as he'd never run before, but he could still hear the wild thumping of his heart, the sound of his boots slapping across the waterlogged liverwort, and the high-pitched chattering of Tikki from deep in his jacket pocket. Fenn had no time now to look out for the windmill, it was all he could do to stumble on blindly through the grass, let alone search for anywhere to hide. Besides, this bit of the marsh was flat and barren; apart from the odd stubby clump of sea thrift, there weren't any trees, nor wrecks. The Malmuts' barks were getting sharper and more desperate; they sounded in pain in their desperation to get him.

Just then, Fenn caught the faint smell of coconut in the salty breeze, carried up from the southern coast. He peered into the distance. A streak of yellow glistened against the grey horizon. It was the last outcrop of gorse he'd seen on Halflin's map – a place to hide. He hurtled towards it, tumbling over his own legs in his scramble. Another bark sounded, even closer. Adrenalin pumped through his heart and suddenly Fenn felt a surge of fresh energy fizzing through his muscles; even though his lungs were burning, he charged over the next few hundred yards. Just as he reached the edge of the thicket, he heard the sound of another Swampscrew, but this one was somewhere ahead.

He plunged into the dense green gorse; if he could get in

deep enough maybe the Malmuts wouldn't be able to get to him, even if they could smell him. There was nowhere else; he had no choice. As he pushed in, he tried to shield his face with his hands and kept his eyes tight shut.

According to the map, the thicket was long but narrow, growing from the bottom of the creek down towards the south coast. Fenn wrapped the scarf around his face and tunnelled inside. Long barbs snagged his scalp but he still didn't make a sound. His life depended on being silent and calm and he forced himself to block out everything. Finally, deep inside the green net of thorns, he stopped stock-still, breathing deep and slow. There was nothing more he could do other than wait and watch, but at least he couldn't hear the barking any more.

Fenn curled his back against the gorse, and poked his fingers into his pocket to give Tikki a stroke. To calm himself, he focused on a stonechat delicately picking its way through the branches, wondering why it was there; a bird wouldn't normally feed at dusk, when owls began hunting. Then, as his eyes got used to the gloom, he noticed there were hundreds of shield bugs swarming over the twigs and the little bird was having a happy time gorging on them. Fenn had only just got his breath under control when he heard the approaching Swampscrew juddering to a halt nearby. He crouched down further, losing himself in the gorse's green tangles and peered out.

A Terra jumped down from the cockpit. It was the young captain from the mudflats. The Swampscrew must have looped across the northern side of the marsh before coming back down to the southern side again. The captain opened up a map and scrutinised it blankly before clicking his fingers to the young boy sent to check for quicksands earlier.

"This it?" he asked him, pointing at the map. The boy nodded. "We camp here!" the captain yelled over the Swampscrew's engine. The engine was cut and the rest of the Terras jumped down, dropping their sleeping mats a stone's throw from the bushes where Fenn hid, scuffing away loose stones and branches to make the ground softer.

"So much for us trapping the kid between us," Fenn heard one of them grumble, as he unfurled his mat.

"The dogs will find 'im in the end. Always do," an older Terra murmured, without bothering to open his eyes as he stretched out on the ground.

"Don't you believe it," the first replied, folding his kit bag under his head for a pillow. "Them new dogs might be fast but they pick up every single smell on this stinkin' marsh. Mate of mine trains them – said they're about as useful as a sponge boat—"

"You two! Stop whinging about nothing and get some kip while you can," the captain barked. "We stick to the plan. If they don't turn up, we'll go find them. Before dawn."

Grumbling about the cold, the Terras prepared for another night in the open. Minutes turned into hours until stars pricked the sky, like velvet punched with holes. Fenn could hardly feel his feet any more, they were so icy, and his fingers burned with the cold, but he still didn't dare move a muscle.

The young boy with the good eyesight was sent to find kindling to start a fire. He trampled noisily around the edge of the gorse before starting to rip dry branches, perilously close to where Fenn was hiding, startling the stonechats from their feeding. Fenn instantly shut his eyes tight – a glint of light on the wet of his eyes would give him away. For a moment or two, he sensed the torchlight skip across his head and he curled his shoulders inwards to make himself as small as possible, the cape's grasses dropping over his head. He opened his eyes and realised the boy had spotlighted the grasses hanging off Fenn's cape.

"There's some kind of nest in…" the boy started, trying to poke the light beam through the gorse's shadows. But before he could probe further, the captain called him back and pointed over the marsh.

"Leave that and help *them*!" he ordered.

Fenn followed the line of the captain's finger. In the distance he could just make out the lights of a small band of Terras, stumbling over tussocks of grass as they lugged something behind them. It was another ten minutes before the men arrived, and despite the icy marsh breeze, sweat had darkened their collars. The Terras who'd already set up camp nodded suspiciously at them as they hauled a willow sledge into view.

At the head of the men were the Malmut trainers, half-dragged by three huge Malmuts, straining so hard against their leashes they made themselves choke on their spiked collars. The trainer with two Malmuts in his charge was red-faced and beefy, his collar pinching his lardy neck, making a ruff of fat. The other was wiry with eyes as sharp as vinegar. Both wore brand-new uniforms, their buttons glinting. Chain-mail gauntlets protected their hands from the jaws of their charges, and leather panels protected their legs. As they arrived, the rest of their troop dropped their backpacks and sagged to the ground.

These Malmuts were different from the ones on the Shanties, longer-legged, with coarse, almost curly fur that grew denser on their legs. They were steel-muscled, ready for the hunt and better fed than the men, although the fat trainer had been helping himself to some of their rations. They could smell fear like an ordinary dog could smell roast meat. They could smell Fenn. As the fat trainer tied them to an ash tree a good distance from the rest of the men, the animals snapped their frothy jaws in the direction of the gorse.

"Stupid dogs! Yapping at every single bird," the trainer snarled, catching sight of the stonechat as it hopped from twig to twig. He quietened them with a smack on their muzzles with his truncheon, before turning back to help the others with a covered bundle on the sledge.

As they braced themselves to drag the bundle over the last clumps of samphire, the cloth fell away to reveal a fourth Malmut. This one was larger than the others, and stared unseeing at the space in front of its eyes, its chest jerking violently as it tried to pant away its pain. A thread of saliva spooled from its mouth, thick as wet wool. The wiry trainer ran to straighten the sledge, fretting as they lumped his dog across the ground.

"Careful with Goliath!" he shouted.

"Boss ain't goin' to be happy with you, Kobel," the fat trainer jeered as he sat down, lolling back on his backpack. Chilstone's orders were always to dispatch anything holding a battalion back – man or Malmut.

"Just givin' 'im a chance to puke 'imself right," Kobel replied irritably. He'd always had a soft spot for Goliath.

"Tell Chilstone that. Word is he's on his way here," the other handler mocked, loosening his collar. The shape of his buttons left a clear imprint in the lardy skin like clay, but seeing the fear flash in Kobel's eyes, he softened. "Get 'im out of the wind, if I were you," he suggested, nodding towards Goliath. "It's biting tonight."

Kobel and two other men lugged Goliath over to the edge of the thicket where Fenn was hiding. Despite being so sick, Goliath instantly picked up Fenn's scent and began whining, but they ignored him. One of the other men let the stretcher thump clumsily to the ground. At this, Goliath lifted his bulky head and his eyes rolled back in his skull. He barked once at the pain in his guts before lolling back.

"Watch it!" Kobel shouted. "You know how much he's worth?"

The Terra gingerly tucked the cloth around the Malmut's rigid body and made to stroke the enormous head.

"He's like royalty!" he said, admiring its collar. Black studs spelt out GOLIATH in the red leather. But before his hand reached its target, Kobel smacked it away with a stick.

"Don't touch 'im!" he shouted, shaking his head at such stupidity. "Fresh out of training that one! He'd take your hand off!"

The other Terra who'd been helping, laughed. "It's half dead!" he said, taking a swig of water from his canteen.

"His jaws ain't," Kobel retorted. "It doesn't matter how sick these boys are. The bite's just a reflex so make sure you..." His voice trailed to nothing as he realised no one was listening. Instead he got out water bowls for the dogs and stomped over to a shallow stream running around the edge of the gorse to fill a bottle.

"His jaws are *greedy*, that's what," the fat trainer said. "If he hadn't eaten that stinking rabbit we'd have been 'ere two hours ago." Kobel ignored him as he filled their bowls. Meanwhile, the fat trainer opened up a log book, and started writing in it. Kobel scowled.

"How about you do their food for—" But he suddenly stopped short and tilted his head to listen out. Over the marsh came a distant whirring.

"Swampscrew!" the trainer said, dropping his log book in panic and buttoning back his collar.

"Chilstone!" another Terra shouted.

The name Chilstone sent the Terras into a frenzy of activity. They re-tied their boots, put their backpacks on and scrambled to standing.

Hearing the name, Fenn's heart felt as if it had been knocked out of his chest, leaving him with nothing but a hollow cell for dread to whistle through, like wind in a crypt.

Chilstone!

He was terrified, but even as the sweat started to crack the thick mud covering his face, he felt the skin-prickling desire to take revenge. The man that killed his grandfather! If only he had a gun, or even a bow and arrow – something he could use from afar. Hunting rabbits and muntjacs with a bow and arrow had been one of the many skills Halflin had promised to teach Fenn, but it always seemed to be something for the following spring.

Thought we'd go next year, Halflin would say, just like he'd said the year before. Fenn knew better than to nag him; Halflin always had a reason why that day wasn't good for teaching Fenn how to hunt.

Too wet; rabbits'll be underground, or if it was dry, *Make hay while the sun shines; I cou' clear ten boats terday.*

Or Fenn had to study. Or a Fearzero might come. Or the wind would carry their scent to any animal worth hunting – or bring wolves to their door. The truth was that Halflin never wanted to teach Fenn to kill. Fenn had been the cause of enough suffering on East Marsh already, even if it wasn't his fault.

Now Fenn kicked himself for not recovering Lundy's harpoon the night the wolves attacked them. If Chilstone was meeting his troops at this spot, he could have got a clean shot through the thicket's thorns. He pulled the rucksack tighter and felt the blade of the billhook press against his back. A billhook could kill a man.

His eyes stung and his mouth was sawdust-dry, as if hatred had drained the sap from him. He'd never even thought of killing anyone before; but now he'd never wanted anything so badly.

7

A Swampscrew appeared, smashing through the far end of the gorse. As it whirred to a halt, muffled commands drifted through the night air. The stonechats flittered silently through the gorse bush and flew off into the night. Fenn strained to see the man he hated through the lattice of twigs, but he could only make out the silhouette of Terra Firma soldiers marching in, trampling the sleeping mats of the other men. These Terras were completely different from any others; they were the elite, well-built and strong, marching in perfect time, stopping at a flawlessly, synchronised point.

Fenn craned to see if it really was the dreaded Chilstone, but the man in their midst was hidden by the bodyguards' bulky shoulders and he could only hear snatches of conversation. Whoever it was was cross-examining Kobel, but his voice was soft and calm. A chill ran up Fenn's spine as he realised it was Chilstone talking.

"It m–must have been off," Kobel stammered. "D–didn't know—"

"The rabbit was poisoned," Chilstone quietly interrupted. Kobel's voice shrivelled to an inaudible whisper. "Your platoon was delayed when you insisted you stop to tend the animal, so you failed to capture the boy. Yes?" Kobel didn't answer.

Fenn strained to see as the guards shuffled out of the way so Chilstone could get a better look at Goliath. Having never heard a physical description of Chilstone before, he was surprised by what he saw; he'd expected someone large enough to match the universal dread of him, someone who looked powerful.

Instead all he saw was a wrinkled old man, so frail and papery he looked like he'd been scraped out, bearing his bent spine's weight on the steel walking stick that he now used to prod Goliath's drowsy eyelids open. Chilstone's skin was the colour of maggots, like the beetle larvae the pigs grubbed out underneath the oaks.

As Fenn gazed, the fear he had always felt at just hearing Chilstone's name fluttered away like wood ash. For years Chilstone's name had made his heart constrict, but he wasn't afraid of the figure standing before him; Chilstone was a shadow of a man who just happened to have an army behind him. Fenn felt his arms tingle as they surged with an unexpected flood of power to match his hate. He could almost feel how his arm would make the billhook swing, the angle its hook would sink in. He took a long, slow breath and gently eased the billhook out of the rucksack.

Chilstone continued to poke Goliath, still limp on the stretcher, bubbles of mucus blowing and bursting from his snout. He worked his way down Goliath's body, first his heaving chest, then his sweating flank. Chilstone didn't speak, which unnerved Kobel even more. He started talking quicker, singing Goliath's praises, saying what a wonderful animal he'd been to train. Hearing his name spoken with kindness, Goliath managed a single weak wag, displaying the enduring canine feature the Terras couldn't quite breed out of Malmut stock: that dogs love to be loved. Goliath whined, and with great effort, lifted his head, but the hemlock was making his already poor vision even worse and he couldn't find the vague silhouette he knew to be his master. Instead he turned and sniffed the hard, cold thing pressing against his cheek.

A bright, white light flashed by Goliath's head. There was a loud bang. A murder of crows scattered from their nearby roost, with caws and jeers, as Goliath's head snapped back. The stretcher was suddenly glazed bright red. Chilstone clipped the holster flap back over his smoking gun.

"The other dogs didn't eat the rabbit?" he enquired pleasantly. He could have been asking the time. Kobel shook his head dumbly and stared at Goliath's lifeless body, unable to comprehend what had just happened. The young Terra who'd helped drag the sledge elbowed him out of his grief and into action. They began bundling up the Malmut's corpse.

"In there will do," Chilstone continued, casually nodding towards the shallow stream. Kobel carried Goliath's body towards the water, dipping his face against his own shoulders to rub the tears from his eyes.

As Fenn watched the scene unfold, he hadn't realised his fingers were tightening around the billhook's handle. In his pocket he found his faithful old penknife and clamped his fingers around that too. He bit his lip. The bodyguards hadn't yet regrouped and he had a clear sight of Chilstone, ten feet away at most. But now Chilstone was slowly hobbling back to the Swampscrew. *It's now or never*, Fenn thought, beginning to push forward as quietly as possible.

Sensing Fenn's tension, Tikki started squirming in his pocket; the racket of the crows circling overhead and the smell of fresh blood had also spooked him. He began a low chattering – the sign he wanted to come out. There was nothing Fenn could do to stop him; he knew from experience that if he tried to hold him back, Tikki would only protest more loudly until he was released. Fenn softly undid the button on the pocket. Immediately Tikki scurried up to the branch nearest Fenn's shoulder, twitching his nose, like he could smell danger. He glanced in the direction Fenn was looking, his fur bristling as he too saw Chilstone for the first time. He stared at Fenn questioningly then scratched at his sleeve as if he wanted to leave, the way he did at the Shanties sometimes, when he'd had enough of rat-catching and wanted to be warm back at the fort.

"No," Fenn mouthed, "stay!"

But Tikki didn't want to. He looked directly at Chilstone again, his fur bushing up as though he'd seen a snake – a mongoose's mortal enemy. Then he crouched down, swaying his haunches, like a cat about to pounce on a mouse. Fenn tried to grab his tail, but just missed. Tikki slipped through his fingertips and scampered through the thicket, flying straight for Chilstone, his claws extended. He landed with a raging screech right on the back of Chilstone's neck.

Before the guards had a chance to react, Tikki ripped his claws in Chilstone's scalp, pulling out a clump of his grey, wispy hair. Chilstone screamed in agony and tripped over his cane onto the ground. The Malmuts barked in a frenzy and leapt forwards, only to have their heads snapped back by their leashes.

"Get it off!" Chilstone yelped.

Chilstone's bodyguards lunged at Tikki, but he had already leapt down and darted between their legs, snapping at their ankles. It was all happening so quickly that Fenn couldn't think straight. Chilstone was lifted to his feet by two of his men who tried to hurry him back to the safety of the Swampscrew. Fenn knew he'd lost his chance; he'd never get close to him now. Meanwhile the trainers tried to release the three barking Malmuts, but their leads were tangled as they fought each other to kill Tikki.

"Run, Tikki!" Fenn whispered.

But Tikki had no intention of running away. Every time he was close to capture, he scampered into the bushes before darting out elsewhere to attack again. Chilstone's guards rushed after him, kicking out and cursing, gradually drawn further and further along the strip of gorse. Fenn suddenly realised Tikki's game: he was trying to draw the Terras away from Fenn. He was trying to save him.

By now, Chilstone had regained his composure, and stood very still throughout the commotion. As Tikki spun by his feet, he darted out his cane, swift as a snake's tongue, and knocked Tikki off balance. For a split second Tikki was on his back, but that was all Chilstone needed. He spiked the cane down on Tikki's chest and pinioned him, then lifted him by the tail. He dangled Tikki in the air to inspect him.

"A mongoose. Must have come in on a Seaborn boat," he murmured. "A prime example of exactly why we must protect our Isles," he continued, holding Tikki in front of the Terras so they could see clearly. Tikki started making a low growling sound. Fenn watched in horror.

"Immigrant creatures such as this," Chilstone continued, "bring diseases. Who knows what other viruses have colonised our shores as the Seaborn race spreads?" He yanked Tikki's tail so hard that the mongoose jolted in the air.

The coiled spring of fury in Fenn's chest snapped, like a watch being overwound. He crashed out of the thicket in a blind rage. A huge thorn twanged back and ripped right across his eye socket, immediately blinding him on one side. He ran screaming at Chilstone, the billhook raised above his head, its long, sloped blade flashing in the lamplight. Blood streamed down his mud-blackened face and the guttural shriek he made was unhuman. Even the most seasoned Terras backed away, remembering ancient tales of marsh demons.

At the same moment, Tikki let out a squeal so unnatural, so high-pitched that it seemed to crack open the night. The crows that had only just resettled skittered up again and heckled the night sky angrily. Tikki arched his back, scrabbled the air as if swimming, then twisted his body so he was facing away from Chilstone. Apart from biting, this particular breed of mongoose only had one other defence mechanism, and Tikki used it now: an arc of fluid shot from Tikki's rear. Fenn rushed at Chilstone.

It was nothing like Fenn had imagined. There was nothing heroic about it. He flailed the billhook blindly and ineffectually, each stroke falling short and hitting thin air. Chilstone wasn't as close as he'd thought, and Fenn suddenly felt weak, the billhook heavier than the logs he used to lug in from the woodshed. He realised he wasn't yelling a terrifying war-cry at all and the childish sobbing he could hear was coming from himself.

Seeing the strange mud-covered creature, like a devil from a swamp, Chilstone shrieked and dropped Tikki. He lost his footing again and fell backwards, clawing at the air for something to hold on to. But his hand only found the sharp edge of Halflin's old billhook as Fenn blindly lashed out.

Two fingers from Chilstone's left hand flew through the air.

The billhook had been Halflin's most valued tool: it cut the reeds for thatch, kindling for fire and butchered meat. To get a new cleaver would have cost him dearly, so he cherished this one, scraping the steel daily on a whetstone so the blade was razor-sharp and it cut clean. So clean, in fact, that Chilstone had a moment's grace when he didn't even feel it, when he didn't realise what Fenn had done to him. It wasn't pain but instinct that made him clutch the stubs of his fingers, his mouth wide open with shock – although he didn't know what he was shocked at. Looking around for clues, he saw his lopped-off fingers rolling to a standstill on the mossy ground and let out a pitiful wail.

Until Fenn heard Chilstone's anguished howl, he hadn't realised what he'd done either. He blinked out the tears blurring his sight and saw red seeping out of Chilstone's closed fist. The Terras stared at him, stunned and strangely static. Time seemed to have frozen. Then Tikki ran up Fenn's leg and down deep into his pocket to hide, squeaking in terror.

Fenn looked first at the blade of the billhook, almost confused about why he was holding it, then at his own hand speckled with Chilstone's blood. Without warning he buckled. Like Halflin, Fenn didn't have the heart to hurt a living thing – not even the monster now trembling before him.

Chilstone staggered back and knocked a lantern over, plunging them all into pitch black as its oil sprayed across the thicket. At that moment there was a sudden thundering of hooves as a dozen wild horses stormed in, herded through the Terras camp by riders cracking whips. One of the horses knocked another lantern and the thicket immediately caught alight. As the flames leapt up, their flickering light showed the terrified Chilstone cowering against the Swampscrew's side still trying to staunch his wounds.

He looked up from cradling his hand and saw Fenn, just a few paces away, the billhook limp in his bloodied hand. For a split second, they stared at each other in shocked silence amidst the chaos; both oblivious to the mayhem around them. Fenn came to his senses first and raised the billhook again, gritting his teeth. Chilstone reached for his gun with his good hand, but just as he pulled it from the holster, a horse galloped between them. The rider reached down and grabbed Fenn by the scruff of the neck, then hauled him up into the saddle. By the time the horse had passed, Fenn had vanished from Chilstone's sight.

8

As they plunged through the burning thicket, the horse's hooves kicked up fiery ash, blinding Fenn. The horse jumped so high that for a few moments Fenn felt as if they were flying, before it landed with a jolt and staggered a few paces as it regained its balance. Fenn heard a metal clatter behind them and realised they had just leapt over the Swampscrew and that the precious billhook must have slipped from his grip and landed on its deck. He tried to work out what was happening by the sounds around him; furious shouts rang out and gunshot split the night air in their wake. Two men fell, lifeless, and their riderless horses ran wildly, catching up with the horses ahead.

As they galloped through the gorse bushes Fenn caught the sound of a Swampscrew somewhere behind them. At this, Fenn's rider whipped his horse even harder, swerving left and right, trying to avoid the bullets whistling past. All at once, Fenn felt an elbow press hard between his shoulders and the rider thrust him down towards the horse's neck to keep Fenn out of range.

They seemed to have lost them but still rode on hard, out onto the murky black swamps, kicking the horses until spit frothed around their mouths and they snorted with exhaustion, their eyes rolling white. There were no proper paths but the horses sensed the way, cantering without hesitation into the black. These horses of the marsh were valued not just for their speed but for their agility in the treacherous bogs.

"Tadey!" Fenn's rider yelled to one of the others at the rear. "Were we dragged?" Fenn carefully rubbed the ash from his eyes on the horse's mane and turned his head to look. A boy, a few years older than him, had pulled the reins short and his horse had come to a jittery halt. He cocked his head, listening intently for a few seconds before nodding.

"Swampscrew. We'll split! Gerran, you take the kid! We'll head them off!" he shouted.

Tadey and the others corralled the riderless horses before disappearing into the night. Gerran yanked his horse to a rearing halt and swerved down into a shallow gulley, where they were hidden by a sea of swaying bulrushes growing along the edges. The horse was tiring and dropped from a gallop to a canter, her hooves slushing the mud.

They rode for another half an hour through the sleet, until a chaffing wind shivered the clouds from the moon and the marsh was bathed in a silvery light. A gleam of water shone like a ribbon of silk in the distance, edged by a long sweep of hunched willows. Gerran stood in his stirrups as they approached.

"Scully!" he called.

A whistle came from ahead and Gerran trotted through the leafy curtains and out onto the bank of an enormous river. There, a guard waited, leaning on a rifle. He wore the same patchwork clothing as Gerran and his hair was braided in the same way as the crew of the *Panimengro*, the Gleaner Fenn had first escaped on. Fenn realised these were Marsh Sargassons, the tribe Chilstone robbed of their children in his hunt for Fenn. They were tall, handsome men, with dark eyes set deep in pallid faces, like their skin had never seen the sun.

Beyond the guard, Fenn could see a narrow causeway, built from tree trunks crossed together and overlaid with willow branches, which led into a mist lying over the river. Gerran's horse danced on her hooves with exhaustion and Scully grabbed her reins while Gerran slackened his grip on Fenn, letting him slip like a sack onto the bank. Fenn crawled away and slumped against a clump of rushes, then gently lifted Tikki from his pocket. But Tikki was too frightened to settle and nipped Fenn's fingers, squirming to get free.

"Who's the kid?" Scully asked, standing over Fenn, the rifle cocked. He put his hand out to see what it was Fenn was nursing, but Fenn shouldered him away, bunching his body protectively over Tikki, still trying to soothe him despite his bites.

"Let him be!" Gerran instructed sharply, turning the horse into the river until she was up to her hocks. "He's had a fright." Gerran leant forward, gently patting the horse's neck while she drank, steam smoking from her silver flanks. "We found him clankin' from the Terras," he said, nodding his head in Fenn's direction.

"At the Punchlock?"

Gerran shook his head. "Couldn't get close to it. Swarming with Terras."

"Think they caught someone?" Scully murmured thoughtfully. Watching how Fenn was crouching, white and shaky in the treacly mud, he relaxed and rested the gun back on his shoulder.

"Nah. Wouldn't still be on the swamp if they had," Gerran said. "I had no squint of Giddock for two moons. Maybe he knows more." Gerran nudged his heel in the horse's ribs and she veered back to the shore. "We heard a shot so went to squint. Found this one in the thick of it."

Fenn watched woozily as Gerran jumped down, rifling through the rucksack. It didn't take him long to find the map.

"This is old," he murmured, unfolding it in the moonlight. "Whoever drew it hasn't trod the marsh a few summers."

As he spoke, Halflin's words drifted back into Fenn's befuddled head. *I've never left the Sunkyard, not fer one night, not in thirteen year.* Halflin must have drawn the map from his mind's eye, from what he remembered of the marsh before he found Fenn; before he was the Punchlock's prisoner.

"Half of this is underwater now," Gerran finished, slapping his knuckles against the paper dismissively. "But the map shows the Sargasson stronghold. Who are you? A spy?" he demanded suspiciously. Fenn curled away from the interrogation. He was too tired to fight any more. He just wanted to be left alone.

"I asked you a question!" Gerran shouted, pulling him up so his feet tiptoed the mud. As his fist made a knot of Fenn's shirt he caught sight of a glint of gold. The famous Demari key, the symbol of Seaborn Resistance. He tore it off in fury.

"Gold?" Scully murmured, elbowing in, reaching out to touch it as it swung glinting in the moonlight. Gerran narrowed his eyes as he studied Fenn.

"Moray will want to see this. Keep an eye out for the others. I'm taking him in before the tide turns."

Gerran stuffed the necklace in his pocket before jumping back on the horse. He reached down and hauled Fenn up in front of him again, then pulled the reins short and steered the horse onto the causeway across the river. Fenn quickly pushed Tikki deep down under his Guernsey where he'd be safe and warm, and held on tightly to the saddle's pommel. The tide was rising quickly and the horse faltered, her hooves twitchy in the wet. Gerran patted her neck and trusting him, she trotted out obediently into the surf sloshing over the timbers. As they rode out further and further, snow began to drift down and for a while Fenn could see nothing as they entered the deep banks of mist swirling up from the water. But after ten minutes the mists began to thin and a gigantic blackened tangle emerged in the distance.

On the far banks of the river, leafless branches snarled up like a giant bramble. It was the forest he'd seen on the map: thousands of brine-dead trees, half-submerged and petrified, forming an island in the middle of a huge river that split one side of the marsh from the other. As they drew nearer, Fenn realised the black, bony trees were spiking out from huge dunes of rubbish; the debris left after the Great Rising, when the trees had acted like a colander through which the huge tsunamis streamed, first inland, then out again, leaving behind smashed-up boats, pylons, buoys, wooden crates, doors and twisted cars.

As they reached the forest, a small wooden landing stage came into view, the frost feathering its deck glinting in the moonlight. Gerran trotted towards the two Sargasson guards, who stood silently, a bark of frost coating their eel-skin hoods. He jumped down and yanked Fenn roughly off the horse.

"Where's my brother?" Gerran asked.

"Watchtower," the second guard replied. "Two Swamp-screws spotted tonight: less than a mile from the borders."

Gerran shoved Fenn up a ladder leading to a platform made out of a flattened car bonnet. From the platform hung a wide bridge made of stripped bark, fixed across two plaited rush ropes. It wove through the rotting tangles of dead trees before disappearing into the thick fog that rolled up from the decaying forest. Weeks of hunting for gulls up in the Shanties' girders meant that Fenn had no fear of heights, but even he hesitated. His left eye was split and he could hardly see out of it. He gently lifted Tikki out again, but Tikki instantly jumped down onto the bridge, scampering a few paces before stopping and checking Fenn was following.

Gerran let out a short, joyless chuckle, like it was the first time he'd tried laughter. "Your little friend has more guts than you!" he murmured.

The bridge was at least sixty feet above the water level, where broken branches thrust up like javelins. Fenn tried to walk very carefully, following the path Tikki took, but each time he stopped on the slimy wood, Gerran gave him a shove. He kept his eyes on the ground the whole time, just managing to dodge out of the way of the lanterns hanging on the branches overhead. Tikki suddenly doubled back and scampered onto the safety of Fenn's shoulder and Fenn felt a short club thump in his chest. He looked up.

Two young boys barred his way, guarding a huge gate made from scraps of metal riveted together – the only way through a high wall of tree trunks, sharpened like pencils. Each boy was also armed with a short-handled, curved sword. Gerran gave them a curt nod and they heaved open the grinding gates, sprinkling them with flakes of rust. Fenn passed into the Sargasson settlement.

He gaped in astonishment. He had thought the whole forest was dead, as Halflin had always told him, but he'd been wrong. Inside its salt-scorched perimeters, a new forest was springing up, at least half as tall as the forest that had been planted years before. In the centre of it all was the Sargassons' fortress; a thick clump of oaks and crack willows grouped densely around a huge sequoia tree, surrounded by another tall ring of wooden spikes. From this, bridges fanned out through the treetops like an enormous spider's web – including the one he was on – with other bridges suspended from them in turn, weaving into the lower branches of the trees or connected with spiralling willow staircases. Hundreds of lights glimmered through the rich green canopy of ferns growing in the damp crowns of the trees. Vines dripped down between the branches, dusted white with the fresh snowfall.

As Fenn walked towards the fortress, he passed dozens of egg-shaped huts made of woven reeds and plastered with mud and reeds from the marsh. They were clustered around the trees like barnacles on a rock. In larger trees, crooked tree houses, built of driftwood, tipped at dangerous angles in the branches, bearing balconies and wonky verandas. He even spotted trees with boats still locked in their branches, rammed there by the force of the waves in the Rising.

On every available space hung troughs, buckets, oil barrels and scooped-out logs planted with herbs, chard, cauliflowers and leeks – protected from the snow with sheets of plastic, or blankets made from bulrush leaves. Gerran noticed the look of wonder on Fenn's face and smiled proudly.

"The Sargassons have grafted to bid life back," he said jerking his head upwards to indicate the birch-bark gutters snaking over their heads for collecting rain. The forest was far from dead, it was a city built from trees, but camouflaged from prying eyes by a circle of death and decay.

The bridge sloped downwards as it looped over the forest, with other bridges branching off from it towards platforms made out of scraps of metal and wood. Fenn passed Sargasson women, all wearing conical leaf hats as they chatted and laughed together, sewing long strips of eel skins to make cloth. On the next platform, men washed and scraped skins of muntjac, beaver and rabbit, dipping them into barrels of white lye to cure them. Further ahead, women and children strung up eel skins to dry over salvaged wire cables from ships and pylons. In the next platform, sopping rubbish was being hoisted up from the dank under-forest below, before being sorted into metal and plastics, just as Fenn had done aboard the *Panimengro*.

Gerran and Fenn climbed up a ladder and dodged around two men testing the strength of a breastplate cut from the side of a steel drum, while peat cutters traded clod cut from the marsh. Most of the people Fenn saw were Sargassons, but he recognised other Seaborn tribes; a few Scotians and Venetians, easily mistaken for Sargassons if their hair was woven in the right style. Fenn saw that none of the children were his age – the generation Chilstone stole.

Fenn couldn't stop staring; to think all this had been on his doorstep and he'd never known. Halflin had known the Sargassons were here, but never knew the forest was an oasis in the sinking marshes. Into Fenn's happiness sidled a cold draught of resentment; if only Halflin had known, then their life needn't have been one of hardship and confinement, ending in death. They could have lived in some kind of comfort. They could even have had friends.

The walkway climbed upwards towards the fortress. After they passed through a gate Gerran pushed Fenn onto a balcony encircling the tree, then shoved open the door cut into its bark and stepped inside.

The tree had been hollowed out but left with enough bark so it could still live. There was a circular room, over ten feet in diameter, with a domed ceiling of wood polished to a honeyed gleam. Fenn imagined it was like being inside a giant beehive; the sweet smell of the sequoia and burning fleabane, used to keep away mosquitoes, hung heavy in the air.

In the centre was a table, cut from a cross section of wood that hung from three chains fixed to the ceiling. There was a series of thin windows like arrow slits that had been hacked out of the tree, then packed tight with small glass bottles glued in with mud. Across the floor, pelts of fox and wolf made a thick carpet. It was warm and smelt of the marsh in spring. As his eyes grew accustomed to the gloom, Fenn realised a lone man sat in the shadows. He stood up as Fenn entered and embraced Gerran. Despite being at least ten years older, it was clear this man was Gerran's brother. His dark hair made him look quite young still but he had a long slab of a face, like a tombstone, with deep set eyes sheltered by heavy brows. Sad, dark eyes, like the windows of a derelict house.

"What d'you see?" Moray asked.

"Terras swarming all over the Punchlock," Gerran replied.

"Thought it was a trap when I saw the *Warspite* had moored," Moray murmured. "Chilstone was waiting for us."

"If his mind was to flush any Resistance out, it didn't work. All we found was this kid. He'd got himself snagged by Chilstone's men."

Moray shrugged indifferently, watching as Fenn stroked Tikki, curled up in his arms.

"Why bring him to me?"

"Found this on him," Gerran revealed, "and a map."

He put the key and the map in Moray's hand. A puzzled expression crumpled Moray's forehead as he looked first at the key, then at Fenn's hunger-pinched face, still staring down at his hands and gently stroking Tikki's back.

"What's his tale? He looks half-dead."

"Hasn't sung," Gerran replied. "No wonder at the fix of him. He took a drubbin'." His face softened as he looked at Fenn shivering, and he lifted a wolfskin from the bench and gently draped it over Fenn's shoulders. Moray frowned.

"Giddock and Scad haven't returned, nor their men," he said bleakly. "You best ride out tonight – check where they're at. Might be they clanked down too if Terras are scoutin' the marsh."

Gerran nodded and the two hugged goodbye. Then the door slammed shut and Moray and Fenn were left alone. Moray slowly turned to gaze at Fenn again, holding out the key. He let the chain trickle through his fingers.

"So who d'you filch this from?" he asked softly. "Think it'd get you passage somewhere?" Fenn tried to grab the key but missed. He felt dizzy and strange. In his mind's eye he kept seeing Chilstone, nursing his hand.

"It's mine," he whispered feebly, steadying himself on the table as the room slid to the left and right. He fixed his focus on the growth rings in the table's wood and stuck out his hand, waiting for Moray to return the key. He was swaying and his bloodstained hand trembled.

Moray took a step closer, looming over him. This kid might look done in, but something marked him out from the other strays the Sargassons had found running from the Terras. Despite his ragged clothes and his skinny frame, he carried himself like a fighter.

"What d'you call yourself?" Moray asked, studying Fenn's face intently. The wound above Fenn's eye had opened up again and blood was trickling down his face. The room suddenly seemed to lurch to one side and he felt too dizzy to stand much longer. He took a breath to quell his sickness.

"Fenn Demari," he said, looking up from Tikki.

Moray sighed. So many had washed up on Sargasson shores claiming to be the last Demari; all of them thinking it would get them special treatment, none of them realising Moray would know if they were telling the truth and not just because of some fake trinket.

"You're a liar."

"I'm not!" Fenn said again, trying to fight off Moray as he fought off dizziness.

There was definitely something different about this one. Moray leant in closer still and gripped Fenn's chin, forcing his face into the light, then cried out and stepped back as if he'd seen a ghost. He hadn't seen those eyes since he'd kissed his friend Maya goodbye, twenty years earlier, when she had been this kid's age. Her eyes were always unmistakable; Moray had never forgotten them.

"It's you!"

Fenn couldn't speak. He suddenly felt very cold as the shock of what he'd been through hit him. Moray grabbed him and held him tightly, laughing and crying at the same time, firing questions at him, calling the guards to get Gerran back. The door opened and someone came in. There was a shout and he heard Chilstone's name again.

Fenn wanted to speak, but his heart was pounding and the rushing sound in his ears was drowning out the rest of Moray's words. He could still see Moray's mouth moving, but couldn't make sense of it. Then everything went black.

9

Fenn tried opening his eyes but something was strapped across them. He managed to sit up and pushed a rough bandage away. He reached up to where the thorn had sliced across his brow and found four twists of what felt like horsetail. He must have been stitched up while he was unconscious.

He was lying on a low truckle bed in the same hollowed room he'd met Moray, although Moray was nowhere to be seen. It was late afternoon and a slab of buttery sunlight fell on the floor through a doorway he hadn't noticed when he first arrived. Outside he could see an orange sky, flecked with birds flying so high they looked no bigger than eyelashes. He pushed the heavy wolf skin off and found Tikki nuzzled down by his side, fast asleep. He gave him a stroke and Tikki yawned widely but didn't wake, smacking his lips as he wriggled back to sleep. Fenn stood up, listing precariously for a few seconds while he tested his balance.

"Wake up, slug-a-bed," he murmured as he lifted Tikki up onto his neck, but Tikki was just as happy to drowse there as well and carried on snoozing.

Next to his bed was a set of Sargasson clothes and his boots, newly lined with soft rabbit skin. Fenn dressed and slid the boots on, then wobbled towards the half-open door. Outside, Moray was standing on a shallow balcony encircled by a stout rail. He was deep in thought as he stared at the setting sun, twiddling something shiny between his fingers. At the sound of Fenn's footfall, he turned and smiled.

"Gave you a dose to help you sleep; the thorns cut deep. I had you needled," he nodded at Fenn's stitches. "You lost a lot of juice, but Mattie did her best. It might not even leave a scar," he said. He held out the sparkling object, "Found this in your shirt." He gestured Fenn to come to his side, then pinned Amber's clover earring in Fenn's pocket before returning his gaze to the forest, scrunching up his eyes against the low golden sun. Fenn followed his gaze, slackjawed with wonder; the whole forest was stretched out before him, and beyond that the rest of East Marsh. Moray smiled to see his eyes widen and pulled open a brass telescope for Fenn to look through. Fenn pressed his good eye against the brass ring and tracked it over the forest.

The Sargasson forest was enormous. Huge swathes of trees had been killed by the brackish water, but there was also a beating heart of green, from which sounds of hammering and voices rose. Towards the south-east all that was left of the forest were a few splintered stumps of trees sticking up like broken teeth. Beyond these, barely visible in the far distance, loomed the long, snaking line of the Wall. They could see people that looked the size of ants working on the last section where the Terras were strengthening it with huge buttresses. It would only be a matter of weeks before it was finished. On the southern shore two dots glinted: the Hellhulks. It was dizzying being so high and Moray reached out his hand to steady Fenn. At the same time he leant over to stroke Tikki's head.

"Your little friend took a chunk out of Mattie's hand before she'd finished stitching. He doesn't like strangers much!" Tikki's lip curled and Moray quickly retracted his hand, smiling.

"You're wise not to trust too quickly, little one," he said calmly, watching Fenn settle Tikki back around his neck. The last of the evening sun glanced off Fenn's face and Moray shook his head sadly.

"You have her eyes."

"Whose?"

"Your mother's."

"You knew her?" Fenn gaped at Moray in disbelief, wincing as the stitches pulled in his skin. He would have to remember not to move his forehead so much. Moray nodded.

"A long time ago."

"How did you know her? What was she like? Did she live here? I don't—" Moray raised his hand to quieten him.

"Too many questions!" he smiled. "I only knew her briefly. She lived here a few years. She was lovely; clever, sweet-tempered, hot-tempered too sometimes."

He laughed at some old memory he wasn't going to share, then looked down at Tikki. "She was good with animals too. She had a way with them. They trusted her."

"She was Sargasson then?" Fenn asked. Instinctively he touched his own black hair; it was black enough to look Sargasson. Moray shrugged sadly.

"What's in a name? My father found her on the shore, nearly water-slain. She was just a bantling, no more than four summers old. Strong though. She'd swum two furlong to shore when a Labour-Ship sank. Even then I knew she'd become someone great. We took her in and believed she had no kin til her thirteenth winter, when kin in New Venice sent for her." Moray sighed as he remembered the unhappy day Maya left his world. "She went before the blossoms came and that was the last time I saw Maya, but I never forgot her." He took the telescope back from Fenn and collapsed it shut, packing away his melancholy as he did. He smiled brightly.

"So, Fenn Demari; your mother was my friend, a stranger, a Sargasson or a Venetian. You pick the story you want…"

"But what about Halflin?" asked Fenn. Moray's smile faded. "He was her father," Fenn explained. "Why wasn't she raised by him?"

"The boat-wrecker was Maya's father?" Moray asked incredulously.

"When Chilstone killed my parents, I was given to him to raise," Fenn explained, unquestioningly repeating the lie Halflin had told him.

"You were raised on East Marsh?" Moray asked, stunned that the Demari child had been close all this time. Fenn nodded.

"All I heard was Halflin's family had been taken to work on one of the Mainland Walls. That was years ago," Moray said, looking over the ocean of forest, shaking his head at the pity of it. "To think Maya was saved and he was here all along. So he kept you hidden for thirteen years?"

"He was afraid Chilstone would come after me, because of being their child. Two months ago, he did," Fenn said flatly, recalling the morning his world flipped upside down. He swallowed back the memory.

An odd look came into Moray's eyes as he watched Fenn fighting back tears. His own boy would have been Fenn's age, had he not drowned in the eel buck his wife hid him in that fateful night when the Terras came. He had reason to hate Fenn Demari, the child that had brought about the death of his own, but all he felt was love for Maya's child and the certainty that he'd never let Chilstone hurt a hair on his head. He hadn't been able to save his own boy, but he could at least protect this one.

"You've been out on the marsh since then?" he asked. The marsh was a hard place to survive, especially alone in midwinter.

"I got on a Gleaner called the *Panimengro*. They saw a patrol ship and dumped me on the Shanties."

"You survived that hellhole?" Moray asked, amazed. He'd known very few who'd ever escaped. "And got back here?"

"The *Warspite* destroyed the Shanties. Me and my friends found a boat."

"Where are they now?"

"West Isle."

"Why didn't you go?"

"I had to light the Punchlock. The Terras came, so I ran," Fenn continued. "They've been hunting me since. Last night they nearly caught me and Tikki..." Fenn's voice cracked with rage. "Chilstone hurt him, and I…" Fenn's lips were white with anger and Moray recognised the same expression Maya had had whenever she witnessed cruelty.

"I didn't mean to…" Fenn faltered.

"What?" asked Moray.

Fenn bit his lip. "I… I cut him…"

"Chilstone's injured?" Moray looked at him in awe.

"I cut his fingers off with Grandad's billhook," Fenn blurted out.

Moray let out a long, low whistle. This scrap of a kid had done that? No one had ever got close enough to hurt Chilstone; he was always surrounded by so many guards.

"He must know you're here," Moray said solemnly, shielding his eyes against the bright light as he looked beyond the forest perimeters. The clouds were melting to orange and purple as they spread across the sun. "He'll come for you."

Fenn shivered, feeling afraid and helpless. His wounded eye suddenly felt so tender and he shrank back from the edge of the balcony, feeling too exposed.

"I'm sorry," Fenn said.

"Don't be, our peace with the Terra Firma was never going to last. Until the attack on the *Warspite*, Chilstone left us alone; he didn't even call us Seaborns. We're nomads of rivers. They call us Bog-men – an insult that protected us."

The muscles at his temple twitched in anger as he

continued to stare into the distance, scanning the sea-charred trees.

"After the *Warspite* was attacked, the Resistance was broken, destroyed. Your parents paid with their lives and the Sargassons paid with their children. Just as no one came to help your parents, no one came to help us. There is no Resistance any more – just what you see here." He turned and looked at Fenn intently.

"The Seaborn tribes have always looked out for themselves. Even on the Hellhulks they still fight each other." He sighed heavily and swept his arm across the forest. "Meanwhile the forest grows again and Terra loggers steal our trees for mine props, while our people are sent to the Hellhulks if they so much as take a bulrush from the marsh. Soon we'll have no home left to defend and no one to help us defend it if we did." He smiled bitterly at Fenn. "You are our only hope. Our last hope. You could bring the tribes together." At that moment there was a creak as the door was pushed open.

"Is the child ready?"

"Mattie!" Moray said warmly, and steered Fenn back into the room.

Inside, a grey-haired old woman waited, wearing a bandage on her hand. She ducked a curtsey as Fenn walked in, running her hands over her shorn hair. Ever since Chilstone took their children, Sargasson women shaved their heads to honour the bereaved mothers. Mattie lit a lamp and pulled up a seat for Fenn to sit on. Moray nodded at her to continue but Mattie hesitated, glancing warily at Tikki. Fenn lifted him down onto his lap where he pretended to sleep while keeping one sneaky eye on Mattie as she lifted a lid from a pail. A lemony smell filled the hut.

"Fleabane for mosquitoes, or they'll eat you alive," Moray said, leaning back in his chair. He folded his arms over his chest while he watched Mattie work.

"How do we stop the Terra Firma?" Fenn asked, as Mattie pulled a horn comb through the knotty tufts of his marsh-matted hair. "Are the Sargassons ready to fight?"

"We have a few guns, but not enough for an army. Bows, beggars' bullets..." Fenn frowned. "Slingshots," Moray explained.

Mattie dragged the comb twice more through the filthy clumps of Fenn's hair before she began picking out the beetles and twigs. Fenn bit his lip, imagining how such a battle would end. Stones against Swampscrews? There would be so many lives lost.

"You proved a boy can fight with nothing but a billhook. Today the hand, tomorrow the head!" Moray said, clenching his fist into a knot. His eyes sparkled for the first time since they began talking.

"Now we have the most important weapon of all: you! Do you hear that?" he asked, jerking his head towards the doorway. From beyond it came a loud hum of voices. Moray stood up and threw open the door. The entire walkway was filling with people, craning their necks to catch a glimpse inside – a glimpse of Fenn Demari. Word had got out, Moray had already made sure of that. He smiled and gently shut the door again.

"You've already started the revolution. Our people want to fight!"

"But you said most of your men have been imprisoned on the Hellhulks?"

Moray nodded. "So in the Hellhulks we have a ready-made army! We need to get word to them that the last Demari is alive. Give them hope. Give them reason to fight the Terras, not each other for the last scrap of bread. They have been waiting for a figurehead. You are the one they'll fight for."

Mattie gently teased the worst of the knots out of Fenn's hair and began to bathe it with the fleabane. Tikki twitched his nose suspiciously at the change in Fenn's scent.

"I've seen how the Terras live. They're sick of the Sweeps, sick of their lives, sick of Chilstone too," Fenn murmured thoughtfully, tilting his head for Mattie to finish washing his hair.

Moray nodded. "Chilstone will be on the *Warspite*, being patched up by his sawbones. This is our chance!"

"But no one can get aboard the *Warspite* without being seen." Rivulets of cold water ran down Fenn's neck, making him shiver.

Moray leant in closer, his eyes shimmering with hatred.

"We don't need to get aboard," he said. "We've been capturing explosives transported from the Fearzeros to the mines. They're packed in a trawler. We're ready to sink the *Warspite* and free the Hellhulks. Then we'll have enough of our men to fight back. And someone to fight for!"

Fenn felt uneasy, remembering the young Terra at the Sweep. He had been cruel and ignorant, but he was young. Surely young enough to change? Mattie gently began braiding his hair into tight plaits, fixing them with stitches using a hawthorn needle threaded with a length of horsehair.

"The means justify the end, Fenn," Moray said, sensing his reluctance. His eyes shimmered with dark bright light as he stared at Fenn. "Agreed?"

Fenn nodded uncertainly, but something twisted in his stomach – a sudden terrible pang of loneliness he'd managed to keep at bay for the past couple of days. He reached up and touched Amber's clover earring, checking it was still in his pocket; he would have given anything to see his friends again, to talk to them. Mattie finished stitching Fenn's hair into the braids and packed away her comb and needle in the pail, then she nodded goodbye to Moray and bobbed Fenn a second curtsey.

"Thank you," Fenn said, reaching up to touch his head for the first time. It felt strange. Moray took a disc of polished brass off a hook on the wall and Fenn peered at his distorted reflection. His hair had been plaited and stitched into coils that wrapped over his head in twirling patterns.

"Now you look like a true Sargasson," Moray smiled. "And even more like your mother." He pulled the necklace out from his pocket and looped it over Fenn's head. "Would you like to see where she lived?" he asked, helping Fenn into a warm muntjac jacket. Fenn nodded as Tikki slipped up again around his shoulders, nuzzling down into the fur.

"Ready?"

Moray opened the door to a chorus of cheers.

10

The evening sunlight glinted off the trees in slanting gilded spurs, making the whole forest shimmer and sparkle. Moray surged ahead, parting a way through the crowds along the walkway, but the bridges still creaked under the weight of people hurrying to see the last Demari. Tides of excited whispers followed in Fenn's wake.

"Where is it?" Fenn asked eagerly as he hurried after Moray down a bridge towards a mass of dark firs in the distance. His heart was galloping. It had never occurred to him he might one day know something about his parents; Halflin had always been so closed off about them.

"When Maya came to us, most of these trees weren't much more than saplings," Moray answered. "In those days we still lived in the old forest. There are still shipwrecks stuck in the trees from the Great Rising. Most are uninhabited now, but in the old days the wrecks were our homes."

The sun loosened snow on the highest boughs and piles of it cascaded down, landing on the walkway in white mounds like wet washing. Undeterred, the crowds did not shift. Fenn was who they'd come to see, they didn't mind getting wet. As they neared the trees, the crowds thickened and the murmuring rose up as people began calling out that the Demari boy had arrived.

"Is he wearing the key?" Fenn heard a man ask, his son riding on his shoulders for a better view.

"I can't see. What's that thing around his neck?" the boy replied.

"An otter?"

"That's never an otter – too small," a woman corrected, poking her head through a gap between two shoulders. Two blushing girls giggled and batted their eyelashes at him as he walked through the crowd.

"They say he attacked a band of Terras!" another woman whispered awestruck as Fenn passed by.

Her friend shook her head sceptically. "But he's just a bairn!"

"Well, you can see the scars!" the first said stoutly.

"I heard he cut Chilstone's hand off!"

"Wouldn't that kill him?"

"That can't be true; he's not even on the marsh ... is he?"

a woman asked, her voice trembling as she tightened her grip on her child's hand.

Fenn wished he could stop and tell them what really happened; that he got the scars from a thorn whipping back in his face, that he hadn't planned to attack Chilstone, that it was a mongoose called Tikki and that Tikki had played a big part in things. But it seemed impossible. Everyone was staring at him like he was a great hero returning from battle.

Someone screamed his name and a couple of "Long live the Demaris!" rang out and suddenly "Long live Fenn!" rippled through the crowds like a wave. A young woman even pushed towards Fenn carrying a baby in her arms. She held the kicking infant up.

"A kiss, please? For luck!" she said, her face glowing with happiness. The baby gurgled with glee as Tikki sniffed his milky breath and Fenn kissed him on the forehead. Instantly the whispered murmurs crescendoed into wild cheers.

Fenn started to feel light-headed, as if he were no longer walking but floating towards the trees. He started to wave back at the crowds, enjoying himself. He shook a few hands. Chilstone and the Terras faded like an old, half-forgotten nightmare; something at the back of his mind rather than something he was ever going to have to face again. His waves unleashed joy from the crowds; there were whoops and shouts, and hands stretched out to touch him and slap him on the back.

It was then he heard the old voice in his ear. At first he tried to block it out. He didn't want to hear it at this very instant, not when everyone was cheering and admiring him. He was having fun for the first time since the night he'd played Truth or Dare with his friends. He waved again, shutting the voice out. But the voice persisted, like an echo had drifted all the way from East Point, needling its way through the trees and crowds, just to single him out and pierce his happiness.

It were pride before fall. That's what Halflin said once, admitting his stupidity in thinking he could outsail a storm and nearly scuppering his boat. A chill ran down Fenn's spine: he realised he still had his storm to sail through. He stowed his hands deep in his pockets out of harm's way and looked down resolutely.

They had reached the inside perimeter of the old forest, where new trees pushed through the wizened old trunks. Moray steered him along the walkway and under an arch of twisting branches. On the other side, in the old forest, Fenn immediately spotted a large barge lodged between the crowns of two huge oaks, slanting at a precarious angle. A circle of younger oaks had grown up around the old trees, so their branches had twisted into and around the boat's hull, hugging the bow tight. The barge had lodged there years before and Moray's father had adapted it to be inhabited, cutting a deeper rectangle around the deck hatch and hanging a door. The boat was high up and the crooked staircase lashed to the trunk made two Zs before it reached the entrance.

"This is where she lived," Moray said, looking up at the topsy-turvy boat. He began to climb the crooked stairs. Fenn swallowed hard. He never thought he'd find out anything about his parents because Halflin had always been so reluctant to talk about them; and now here he was, about to see where his mother had grown up. He had just gripped the rail to follow, when a commotion further along the walkway made him stop and turn round. The crowds turned to see as well, and a few voices were raised as someone demanded to be let through.

Fenn peered above their heads to find out what was happening. In the dark shadows he spied a glimpse of silver, like the flash of a fin – the luminous strip on the jackets the Terras sometimes wore. Someone was pushing their way through the crowds. Fenn glimpsed a tuft of bright red hair and his heart jolted like it had missed its footing.

"Fenn!"

It was Amber, storming through the crowds towards him, shoving people out of the way, not caring who she elbowed in her haste to get to Fenn. Behind her he could see Fathom waving and grinning, and further back, Gulper jumping up and down wildly as he tried to see above the crowds. Fenn charged forward to meet them, thrusting through the jumble of bodies barring his way. He heard Moray shout something behind him as he skidded back down the stairs to catch up, but that was just noise to Fenn. All he cared about was reaching his friends, giddy with delight. "Sorrys" were spilling out of his mouth as he barged through the crowds, stamping on toes, but he didn't slow down until suddenly he was there. *They* were there. He was with his friends.

Then it was a mash of hugs and Amber's "Oh my Gods!" and Tikki slid off his neck into Comfort's arms as she clung to Fenn's legs, like a limpet that could never be loosened by the tide. And all he wanted to say was, *I missed you!* but the words kept getting lost, so each time he opened his mouth, he simply shut it again.

"You know them?" Moray asked incredulously when he caught up. "This lot got picked up the day before you came!"

"These are..." Fenn at last managed to blurt, but joy choked up his throat. He began laughing and shaking his head in disbelief. He swallowed hard and tried again. "These are my friends!"

Gulper now had him in a bear hug that was crushing all the air out of him.

"*Friends*," Gulper said, practically snuffling like a pig that's found truffles as he basked in the reflected glory. "My good friend!" he whispered, tears in his eyes too. He only released Fenn because Amber had barged in. She grabbed his shoulders and yanked him round to face her. Then, half-shaking, half-squeezing him, she gabbled a hundred questions at him, punctuated with tellings-off.

"Fathom told us who you really are! Why didn't you ever say? Didn't you trust us? How did you end up here? Someone said Chilstone caught you! How did you escape?" She paused and drew just enough breath to fuel the next barrage of questions. "Why didn't you say what you were going to do? We could have helped! It was so dangerous! What do you think you were doing?" She prodded Fathom sharply in the shoulder. "That's all everyone is talking about, isn't it Fathom?" she said, without waiting for him to answer. "That you lit your grandad's Punchlock! That was so stupid! Incredibly stupid! You could have... You could have got yourself killed! You—"

She came to an abrupt halt, like something had stuck in her throat and she had such a look in her eyes, such a wounded look, that Fenn couldn't meet her gaze.

"I do trust you..." he at last managed, but before he could

say more, Moray had raised his arms and two Sargasson guards ran up to keep the crowds in check.

"Inside," Moray ordered, steering the children towards the barge. He was afraid that Fenn might be overheard saying Chilstone was on the marsh; he didn't want a panic. The children climbed up the stairs.

"This was where Maya used to live," he explained as he threw open the door.

"Your mum?!" interrupted Amber, her eyebrows travelling even higher up her forehead. "Your mum lived here? I never knew she was Sargasson! So that's something else…"

"I didn't know either – and she wasn't Sargasson … well, not exactly," said Fenn, defending himself from further accusations of secrecy. "Let's just get inside. We can talk there."

The sun had now set and it was too dark to see much inside, other than that they were in a small, boxy room that sloped acutely to one side. Moray lit the lamp on the wall and as the flame bulged, the room showed its secrets.

It had been painted a shade of blue-green, the colour of the sea, and across the ceiling and walls were hundreds of multicoloured fish, swimming between forests of seaweed that had been intricately sketched around every porthole. Against the far wall was a ladder made from thin branches lashed together with strips of leather. It led through a hole cut into what had once been a dividing wall, but because of the boat's angle, was now a ceiling. In the middle of the room was a table cut from a round of wood, with tree stumps for stools around it, and a small, green enamel stove.

"This was all your mother's work," Moray explained as he knelt and lit the kindling stacked in the stove. Firelight flickered on the walls, so the seaweed and fish seemed to dance. Amber stared entranced, tracing her fingers over the shimmering fish and turquoise shells, temporarily forgetting her torrent of questions.

"It's so beautiful," she whispered.

Fenn sat down heavily.

"It's a lot to take in," Moray said softly as the children blinked at their surroundings. He looked gently at Fenn. "And you've been through a lot – more than most grown men. You need to rest."

He turned to the others.

"Don't worry about your things. I'll see you get your stuff brought over," he explained as he laid a log on the crackling fire. "There's room for you all here." He nodded his head towards the ladder as he stood and dusted down his hands. Then he laid his hand on Fenn's shoulder for a few seconds before opening the door again.

"You'll look after him," he said solemnly to Fathom, who had found a blanket and was already draping it over Fenn's shoulders, then he stepped out into the dusk. "We'll talk more tomorrow, when you've rested."

As soon as the door swung shut, Amber sat down by Fenn's side. Comfort lay her head on Amber's shoulder and Amber put her arm around her. She gently tickled Tikki, who padded around in her lap in many small circles until he found the right spot, and then curled into a ball, with his tail over his face for a bit of peace and quiet. For a few moments, the children simply sat in silence, letting the tranquillity of Maya's paintings wrap around them. Gulper was the first to speak.

"Well, let's see it then!" he demanded, slapping his hand on the table and nodding at the hint of gold sparkling around Fenn's neck. Fenn shuffled off his dazed state, unhooked the chain and handed it over.

"Oh. I thought it'd be bigger!" Gulper mumbled, frowning and clearly dissatisfied as he passed it to Fathom to inspect.

"Well, very sorry to disappoint you," Fenn laughed, as Amber gave Gulper a cuff around the head before putting out her hand to see the key too. She dangled it between her fingers while Comfort tapped the key to make it spin.

"It's so lovely. Do you know who made it?" she asked. Fenn shrugged as he put it back on. "I'd love to have something of my mum's," she said wistfully, watching him. The truth was, Fenn didn't know quite what he felt for someone he never knew; even the word "Mum" was just a word to him. He'd never used the word as a name; there was never an actual person. But it was different for Amber.

She'd never even known her dad, but remembered enough of her mother to also know how much she must have forgotten. It was like she had done a jigsaw puzzle years before and still had a few dog-eared pieces from it, but with no idea where they belonged. Sometimes the memories she clung to only showed her how much she'd lost, and hurt more. Fenn clicked the catch of the chain back, noticing how her face hollowed; that always happened when she bit the inside of her cheeks to stop herself crying. He put his arm around her shoulders and gave them a squeeze, and she almost flinched, as if she wanted to be alone with her sorrow.

"You were meant to be in West Isle!" he said, changing the subject. Amber swallowed back her tears and tried to smile.

"We saw the *Warspite*—"

"Saw it? Nearly mowed us down!" Gulper interrupted. "The *Madeleine* tipped so bad she started takin' water. But we hobbled back to shore, thanks to Fathom." Fathom smiled at the compliment. "We nearly died!" Gulper's eyes bulged out at their bad luck.

"We got picked up by the Sargassons. They were out

looking for whoever lit the Punchlock," Fathom continued.

At this, Amber gave Fenn a pointed look as she cut in. "We *knew* it was you, but we didn't say anything."

"We didn't know if we could trust them," Fathom explained.

"An' thought we'd be flyin' up your ointment if we said who you were. So we kept schtum," Gulper said. "Anyway, what about you?!"

Fenn was halfway through telling them about his race across the marsh and everything Moray had told him, when they were interrupted by a knock at the door. A Sargasson boy was waiting outside. He came in, carrying two huge tiffin boxes in a yoke over his neck. He unstacked the pots and put them on the table. The whole time he was there, he gawped wide-eyed at Fenn, a dopey smile on his lips. He was so spellbound he kept knocking over plates and he walked straight into the wall instead of the door on his way out.

"You're going to be treated like a king here. The last Demari!" Amber remarked as she lifted the lid of the first tiffin. "You can see why people pretend to be you," she said.

But Fenn was tired of being Fenn Demari. He was exhausted and starving; he just wanted to eat. "This smells good!" he said hurriedly, loosening the other lids. A delicious smell filled the cabin.

Inside the boxes there was a golden roast chicken and two braised pheasants, buttery rice speckled with herbs, roasted chestnuts, samphire, scorched white chunks of eel pierced with skewers of rosemary and a glossy stew of venison that melted in their mouths. To mop it all up were loaves of soft coconut bread, and six prized potatoes that must have been grown in the troughs Fenn had seen on the way in; steaming hot and fluffy, and dusty from the wood ash they'd been baked in. In the last two tiffin they found sweet, chewy cakes made from crystallised apples and honey, and blackberries pureed into a thick jelly the colour of amethysts. There was also a bottle of a ruby-red rosehip cordial that seemed to soothe all their aches and pains away, and tingled in their stomachs more than the hot food.

For the last few days, all Fenn had eaten were bulrush seeds and a few oats – surviving on supplies that wouldn't have staved off hunger for a day. He'd run hard, been soaked through and viciously bloodied by hawthorn barbs. He was already thin when he'd arrived back at East Marsh, but the last few days had brought him to the shores of starvation. As the rich smells wafted up, Fenn was close to fainting; and as each delicious mouthful went down, he felt like he'd never be able to stop eating. He remembered parts of himself he'd long forgotten; the basin of his stomach weighted, the muscles in his throat stretched again. The simple sense of swallowing felt luxuriant.

"You need to slow down," Amber said thoughtfully as she watched him wolf down three chunks of venison.

But as far as Fenn was concerned, he couldn't go fast enough. He lifted the bowl to be nearer his mouth – no point in losing time for the spoon to travel – and he shovelled it in. Before he'd started he hadn't realised how hungry he was, but now he was licking the bowl; he was going to leave nothing. It was only as he scooped in the last mouthful that he felt his stomach start to strain, like a stretched drum.

"Stop," Amber said firmly, "it's time for bed." She pulled the bowl out of his greedy grip, not remembering that those words were exactly the ones her own mother used with her on the rare occasions they got something to eat.

Fathom and Gulper helped Fenn up the rickety ladder that led up to the next room. They pushed open the door in the floor and Fenn went through. Like the room below, the floor was at a tilt and at the far end was a second ladder leading up into the topmost room. On one wall, Maya had begun a painting of a mermaid combing her golden hair as she leant aginst a coral reef. Beneath the portholes of the old boat, two low beds were heaped with pillows stuffed with bulrush heads, and there were thick beaver furs and coarse linen blankets. It was snowing hard outside and the last of the light coming through the round window was tinted turquoise. They could see their breath steaming as they lit the lamps.

"It'll be warmer on this floor," Fathom said. "Me and Gulper can sleep up there." He nodded towards the second ladder and heaped a load of blankets into Gulper's arms to carry up. "We'd better wrap up warm; it's going to be freezing tonight."

Fenn was limp with tiredness and his eye still throbbed. Fathom gently pulled off his boots and dragged the covers over him, then Tikki slid out of Comfort's arms to wriggle down next to him, curling into the crook of his neck, where he began to purr contentedly. Amber and Comfort clambered into the other bed, lying top to toe, and the boys disappeared into the room above.

"Goodnight," Amber whispered into the dark, but no one was left awake to hear her. She curled over, trying to remember every memory she had of her mum, going through them one by one to pin them down as firmly as she could. Soon they were all deep asleep, with not a sound in their dreams but the robins singing outside in the falling snow.

11

Fenn slept until nearly noon the next day, and when he woke he refused to open his eyes. He knew it all had to have been a dream, but he didn't want to leave. He must have wanted to see his friends so much again he'd actually dreamt it; he must have been so starved, he'd dreamt they'd gorged themselves on crispy roast chicken and fluffy potatoes, then stuffed down blackberry jelly, turning their tongues purple.

But it was strange how he could almost taste the blackberries. Then he smelt something smoky, and felt something move by his face. He blinked open his eyes and found Tikki sitting next to him on the pillow, a half-chewed potato skin in his paws. On the floor was a stone-cold mug of tea, brewed from blackberry leaves that Amber had brought up earlier. Fenn sat up and rubbed a spyhole in the ice that caked the porthole by his bed. Outside, the forest was blanketed in thick snow and the sun sparkled high in the sky. He could hear soft *flumps* as melting snow cascaded off roofs and firs, and the sound of his friends chatting drifted up from the room downstairs. He felt like his heart was going to burst with joy as he slid out of bed, pushing the blanket of beaver skins to one side. He pulled on his boots, lifted open the door to the room below and climbed down.

"Hey, slug-a-bed!" called Fathom as Fenn stepped down through the hatch.

Gulper and Comfort were sitting on piled-up furs next to the stove, where Amber was poking at the contents of a skillet. Gulper had his foot crooked around in his lap and a small penknife in his hand; he was trying to pare down his filthy toenails that had grown long and ragged. As soon as Fenn came in, Comfort jumped up and hugged him, before gently taking Tikki and tucking him into her lap. Gulper budged up to give Fenn the warmest spot.

"Here he is!" said Gulper grandly as Fenn sat down.

"The last Demari!" Amber teased. She splashed a little water from a cup into the skillet and gave it a thoughtful stir. Fenn blushed red. He'd never meant to lie to his friends.

"Well, now the secret's out good and proper," Fathom said. "There were gangs of kids outside this morning. Been there since dawn, trying to catch a glimpse of you! Moray had to clear them off."

"Moray was here?" Fenn asked.

"Wanted to see you, but you were out for the count," Fathom said.

"He wants to know exactly what you saw on the marsh," Amber said, as she stirred the skillet again.

"Lots of his men haven't returned," Fathom explained.

"I saw lots of Terras. And Chilstone," Fenn said, grimacing. And suddenly there they were, back in his mind's eye: Chilstone's fingers spinning through the air. Amber noticed his face clouding.

"Anyway, he said he'd be back later, so we've got the rest of the day to ourselves," she said over brightly. "And *you* need breakfast."

She began doling out hot fried rice, mixed with flakes of smoky fish and boiled eggs. A spicy smell rose up and Fenn's mouth started watering. "The kid that brought it called it keggery," she explained airily, showing off her new-found knowledge as she dipped the spoon in for another helping.

"Though' he said kedgeree?" Gulper asked, switching feet as he began neatening up the next sty of piggies.

Amber shook her head emphatically. "Keggery." She tipped some more rice into the bowl. "You're going to love this, Fenn. It's delicious, isn't it, boys?"

Gulper and Fathom nodded as she pronged an extra-large

chunk of fish and knocked it into the bowl, slipping Fenn a soft look. He eyed the bowl greedily.

"Actually, I thought he said kedgeree, too," Fathom said after a moment's thought.

"No, it was definitely keggery," Amber insisted. There was a hint of a slap in her voice. She had stopped ladling the food but still had Fenn's bowl in her hand. Fenn watched as tantalising spirals of steam wafted up.

"You sure?" Gulper asked, abandoning his pedicure for the argument, "because I think I've heard of it before and—"

"I know what I heard, Gulper!" Amber snapped. "I was the one he gave it to..."

She still had the bowl in her grip. The scented steam wafted down in Fenn's direction. He reached up his hands hopefully.

"Yeah, but we were both just behind you." Fathom looked at Gulper for confirmation.

"That's right, and there's two of us..." Gulper stuck out his lip.

"Can I..." Fenn started, but Amber wasn't listening to Fenn. A point was to be made and she was the one to make it.

"And there's two of us too," she said, looking at Comfort. "You thought he said keggery, didn't you?"

Comfort had been watching Fenn during the children's argument, but now she gently put the sleeping Tikki in a little nest of fur next to her and stepped over Gulper to reach Amber. Taking this to mean solidarity, Amber gave Fathom and Gulper a smug look, followed by a little nod of triumph. But before she could crow, Comfort prised Fenn's bowl out of her hands and gave Fenn his long awaited breakfast.

"*Thank you*, Comfort!" Fenn said and began tucking in.

"Sorry!" Amber exclaimed as she realised.

"It's fine – Comfort looked after me!" he said, laughing at their worried faces.

Comfort smiled to hear her name and came back to sit with Tikki while Amber shoved a foot into one of her huge boots.

As she yanked her laces tight, Fenn just caught her say, "It *was* keggery," under her breath, but if Gulper and Fathom heard too, they weren't going to bother fighting any more. Amber never gave up; it was her best and worst feature. Instead, pedicure over, Gulper pulled his socks back on – so holey that his toes all poked through the ends, like they were sleeves rather than socks and he wiggled them disconsolately. Fathom grabbed his coat off a nail on the door and looked outside.

"Snowing again," he said as the porthole speckled with white flakes. "Better wrap up." Amber nodded as she wound her laces tight around her boots.

"S'posed to be water snakes down in the rubbish dunes," she explained, when she caught Fenn's puzzled look.

"Where are you going?" he asked, dropping his spoon back in the bowl. He'd already finished the lot. Amber glanced uneasily at Fathom, shuffling her feet.

"When they brought us in..." she faltered. Fenn's heart sank to see that old look back in her eyes – two splinters of ice that warm fires couldn't melt. "There's an old lady," she mumbled, looking at the floor, stubbing the toe of her hobnailed boot into the rush mat. "Lives on the edge of the forest..."

"She draws missing people," Fathom explained. "You know, people who've got separated on convoy ships, that sort of thing. Amber thought she might get some clue about her mum. And I might find Neva, my sister."

There was something in Fathom's eyes, like he was almost embarrassed about the idea. He knew it was absurd to hope – he'd let go of Neva's hand two years before, in the pitch-blackness on a sinking ship. He was also sure Amber couldn't even remember what her mum looked like. He'd asked her once and she told him to mind his own business with such a slicing voice that he never dared mention it again. But Fenn saw beyond the bleak desperation; he just saw the desperate hope.

"I'll come," he said, wanting to at least be part of their optimism – seeing as he had none of his own. Even a speck of hope was better than the yawning feeling he felt whenever he thought of a future without Halflin. "Tikki?" he called, as he pulled on his coat.

Tikki peeped slyly out of the corner of his eyes before quickly closing them again and pretending to be asleep. Comfort's lap was warm. Outside was not.

"I'll stay and look after Comfort," Gulper quickly said, washing his hands in the heat of the brazier as he spread out into the warm space Fenn had left. The fire was warm. Outside was not. Gulper happily wriggled down into the furs and prepared for a snooze. Comfort drew out a little packet she must have had hidden away and took out a threaded needle; and with the socks still on Gulper's feet, she carefully began to stitch up the holes.

"You could do that yourself, you know!" Amber said sharply, but Gulper just smiled and leant back on the furs, wiggling his toes at her.

They closed the door behind them and tramped out onto the snowy walkways, bundled up with fur hats and mufflers, heading towards one of the gateways in the high wall that surrounded the settlement. The heavy snow had kept everyone indoors, so the children were entirely alone as they trudged out. At last they reached the gate and knocked, thumping the flats of their hands against the metal patch-work. A small hatch opened in the centre, framing a pair of eyes peering through. As soon as he recognised it was Fenn, the guard instantly opened the gates, insisting on shaking Fenn's hand and clapping him on the back before he let them pass.

Half a dozen ladders led off that first walkway and into the under-forest, but after a few minutes Amber recognised the point where they had been brought up by the strange shape of two fallen boughs. How Amber remembered the way amazed Fenn, but then he recalled that she'd known every shortcut on the Shanties; she had an instinct for direction.

It was still only mid-afternoon but it might as well have been night-time down on the rubbish dunes, because the walkways and branches above them blotted out most of the sunlight. Fathom lit a lantern, hung it from the cleft in a long branch and led the way as they carefully tramped across the pontoons – wooden bridges made from barrels floating in the water. Here and there they passed small groups of Grubbers and Toshers whose job it was to pick through the rubbish, looking for anything useful that had washed up in the forest. They collected bits of metal and plastic that could be reused while the youngest Sargasson children ran, banging metal lids with sticks to scare off water snakes.

Ferns and ivy were gradually colonising the rotting trees, and tiny self-seeded oaks and maples were sprouting waist-high through the dead snags. When the children left the pontoons to wade through the undergrowth, hundreds of frogs and toads leapt around their feet.

"Urrgh!" shuddered Amber. "Why are there so many of them?"

Fenn looked puzzled: they should have been hibernating, especially in this weather. He remembered the insects crawling up the willow tree. Something was out of kilter on the marsh this winter. They pushed on, but progress was slow and difficult, until at last Amber held her hand up.

"Shh," she whispered. "We're nearly there."

A faint rattling sounded through the darkness, like a rattlesnake's tail. Amber stood stock still, listening for its direction, before darting forwards again through the low elderberry bushes and alders. The jangling got louder, reminding Fenn of the noise the sunk-marked boats used to make, waiting for the Punchlock, the tinny clamour of the steel sail hoists banging against the masts. They clambered up a bank of rotten logs, thick with moss and suddenly it came into view, like the shimmering sail of a ghost ship.

"That's it," cried Amber racing ahead. "Come on!"

Ahead, a giant curtain was strung up through the trees like a huge web, with thick anchor lines fixed to the branches of the tallest dead firs. To see the very top, they had to tilt their heads back so far it hurt their throats. It had been made out of rubbish; fishing nets, sails, lengths of plastic tape and barbed wire snaffled from the Terra Firma fences. Sewn, stapled and tied into it were thousands of discs of tin and plastic, silver-birch bark and even oyster shells, all shimmering and rattling in the breeze. On every single disc there were little portraits engraved, often on both sides: the person seeking, the person missing. Amber grabbed one.

"Davia," she read out loud. "Eight years old." She turned it over and read the back inscription. "My daddy is Marin." She looked over her shoulder at Fathom and Fenn. "The poor little thing must be looking for her dad. Wonder if she found him." She let go of the disc and picked up another, reading it to herself this time. "So you see?" she declared. "My mum might have come this way too. I could still find her!"

Fenn looked at the curtain doubtfully; there were thousands of faces staring at him through the gloom, their discs jangling in the breeze.

"I'm going to look for Neva!" Fathom said, beginning to read the discs.

Amber flitted quickly along the curtain, making the discs clatter as she shuffled through them. She reached the end and turned back, so fast that she couldn't have been looking properly.

"Can you really read them like that?" Fenn asked gently. She came to an abrupt halt, and spun around to face him.

"Oh, you noticed, did you? Yes, there are loads to get through," she replied, her voice brittle and sharp. "And you could help!"

Fenn walked over to her side. "So what's her name?" he asked, starting to look through the discs.

Amber suddenly hesitated, like she'd had the wind taken out of her. "Her name was…" She looked at Fathom for help, but he couldn't. Then she stared at Fenn in confused sadness, shaking her head at him as if he'd wronged her. She'd forgotten. "It'll have *my* name, won't it?" she snapped, flipping through more of the discs, her neck colouring up with the shame of not knowing what her mother had been called.

She hurried on along the curtain, peering intently at each image, then paused in mid-flow and held a disc up for Fenn to see. "What's the V stand for?" She asked him directly, as if he knew. It was as if she expected him to know everything.

"Venice?" he ventured.

A rustling came from the tree overhead and a thin, sugary voice seeped down, its notes swinging sadly like the pendulum of a clock slowly running down. It was hard to tell if it was man, woman or child.

"That's right! But they should all be Ls…" the voice sang.

"L for lost ... losers, weepers," it continued, warbling sadly.

Fenn peered at the dark patch above where the voice had treacled out.

"It's her!" Amber whispered, her eyes huge as she searched the shadows above.

They could just make out the silhouette of someone squatting above them, where scraps of wood had been assembled to make a platform with sheets of plastic draped over it. The tree trunk had a bucket handle, lumps of wood and bicycle handlebars nailed up it, acting as a ladder.

A head unexpectedly poked out, making them jump; a woman, practically bald, save for some scraggy tassels of hair. She was gnome-like, with a head that looked too heavy for the thin stalk of her neck. She wore a dark green dress that might have once been velvet, although most of the nap had rubbed away.

"Looking for someone or someone looking for you?" she trilled as she stretched her neck out further. She smiled, her mouth wet-lipped and red as a worm. "I'm Scratch; face-maker, make-a-face, faker-maker, make-a-fake," she sang. "Sisters look for brothers, dogs look for fleas, youngs look for olds, trees look for leaves."

The rest of Scratch's body followed her head as she crept out along the branch. She was long-legged and long-armed, and she dangled upside down for a moment beneath her treehouse like a crane-fly. Her hair was stringy and hung down as she swung. After a few moments she let out a bored sigh, then hopped back into her hut and peeped out at the children, her frail knees drawn up under her chin.

"Looking's nothing, drawing's something," she chirruped.

"How can I find my sister?" asked Fathom. "There are thousands of them!"

"Do I look like a detective?" Scratch snapped with a withering glare. She sniffed. "Look yourself! Stay a day, stay a week. Stay as long as you want to seek."

She laughed childishly and folded up her spindly arms, while she waited for them to answer. Her eyes gleamed brightly in the gloom and she rocked back on her heels, looking down quizzically, like a blackbird eyeing up a worm.

"If you'll be patron, I'll take paying," she chirped, sliding down the side of the screen to see them better. She fell the last few feet, and landed with a bump on the soft moss beneath her tree.

Scratch stood up and brushed herself down, fastidiously plucking off leaves that had caught on her dress; she was clearly very vain. Then, delicately picking up the hem between her thumb and finger so her dress didn't scrape in the dirt, she took a dainty step towards the children, sashaying through the gloom.

When she reached them she clicked her fingers to show she wanted to see some food for her efforts. Her fingertips were blackened by the charcoal she used, and blistered from scratching on the pieces of tin. She suddenly shivered and wrapped her arms around herself, rubbing herself warm.

"The evening's cold or I am old," she whispered, with sudden deep melancholy, as if she'd only just realised how ancient she was. She grabbed handfuls of dry leaves banked against a tree trunk, rolled them into balls and stuffed them beneath her dress – the same trick Halflin had taught Fenn one bone-snapping cold winter. The more she packed in, the more like a pot-bellied spider she looked. When she'd finished, tufts of moss sprouted at her neck like a ruff.

"How much?" asked Amber. Scratch sucked her teeth and gazed at her with her bright enquiring eyes and as her expression softened, a gentle smile expanded across her face.

"On the house for you, sweet cheeks," she said, before suddenly giving Amber's face an unexpected sharp slap. "But don't get all weepy on me now! I can't abide boo-hoo-hoos!"

Amber reeled, too shocked to react, and just looked at Fathom and Fenn in bewilderment. Scratch delved into the pocket of her apron, an ancient old shirt, stiff with paint, and pulled out a piece of plastic cut into a disc.

All the tools of her trade came from here: several styluses, made of bent nails or flint, clay pots of charcoal and red alder root; a stiff brush to work in the colours and finally a pot of raw egg white she used to glaze and fix the paint. The pads of her fingertips were her palette, stained with each pigment. Her little finger on her right hand was bright red from alder root for lips, on her left hand, blue from woad, to colour in eyes. Amber sat down next to her and began to describe her mother so that Scratch could make her portrait.

As Fenn listened, he realised that Scratch wasn't selling anything other than hope. She could just about draw a vague image to support the recollections of people who had long forgotten the faces of those still breaking their hearts. That was her skill. Of all the thousands of portraits fluttering in the wind that evening, none was fluttering so violently as the anticipation in Amber's heart. Fenn looked over Amber's shoulder at the little disc she nursed in her hand, like a fledging fallen from its nest.

"Looks just like her," Amber whispered as she gazed at the image – the dark eyebrows, a full mouth, the bright green eyes. On the back Scratch had gouged, *Mum. Looking for you. Amber. 14.*

"This is a good spot," Scratch told her, taking the disc back to clip up on the batch that had been newly hung. Like a freshly planted part of a cemetery, the colours on these portraits were bright. "You'll never miss it here."

Scratch stowed her painting tools back in her apron

pocket, hunching over herself secretively as if Fenn and Fathom were thieves. Fenn returned to examining the portraits. Most were faded, becoming white shards of plastic as their pigments floated off in the forest mists. Just like the Seaborns, Fenn thought: a people disappearing, forgotten, drifting away. He thought of Moray's words to him the day before. *You are our only hope. Our last hope, you could bring the tribes together.* It was down to him.

Just then a breeze slithered through the trees, making the flame of Fathom's lamp stutter and shiver, then go out. As he relit it, Fenn felt a sudden chill creep under his skin. Scratch seemed to sense it too and scurried back up to her treehouse.

"Lost son, the hidden one," she sang as she climbed. "One, two, I know it's *you!*" Breathlessly she scrambled into the safety of her hut. From inside, Fenn could still hear her nervously singing her song in a weepy whisper.

"Three, four, death's at your door!"

Through a crack in the hut's slats, he could just see Scratch's eyes peeping out fearfully as she scanned the trees outside.

"What do you mean?" he called up. Scratch leant out cautiously and peered out. She pointed a single trembling finger towards the distant marsh.

"Five, six, down on sticks!" Her voice was ragged as if she

was very scared. "Seven, eight, they're at the gate! They're at the gate!" She let out a little squeak of fear, then hopped back inside her shack, like a cuckoo in a clock, and slammed the door shut.

"Mad as a box of frogs," Fathom murmured, shaking his head and laughing to himself. But Fenn still stared after her and shuddered.

"She's warning us. I just don't know what about."

12

Dusk fell further on the dunes and Fathom's lantern only pooled enough light to see a few feet ahead. Walking back was even slower than before. They were about to clamber over a rotten elm, blocking their path, when Amber stopped dead in her tracks.

"D'you hear that?" she asked. She tilted her head to listen beyond the sounds of the Grubbers and Toshers packing up for the night. "I thought I heard something." Fenn strained to hear but couldn't catch anything other than the sound of the tide sweeping in.

"Can't you hear it?" Amber insisted. "It's coming from over there," she pointed through the trees, out towards the river.

Fenn shimmied up into the fallen elm's to see. The wind whistled through it's branches making the dead leaves rustle, but he still caught it: the sound of whinnying from far beyond the edge of the forest. He peered through the snags. He could just see the end of the causeway from here. The crossing had not yet been submerged by high tide, but waves were just beginning to break white against the hundreds of enormous tree trunks laid across to the far side of the water, invisible behind a solid bank of river mist. Suddenly out of the grey spray he caught sight of the source of the noise: a horse was thundering at breakneck speed along the causeway, headed for them.

"Who's that?" Fathom asked, climbing up beside him. "Thought Sargassons were master horsemen – he's riding like a maniac!"

Fenn stared through the fog. The rider seemed to be slumped over the horse's neck.

"Something's wrong!" he shouted, jumping down.

They all scrambled towards the river, skidding and leaping over the collapsing rubbish heaps towards the water's edge. Faster than the others, Fenn was first on the causeway.

The horse suddenly stopped galloping, and started bucking instead. The rider still didn't seem able to get her under control, although he was clinging on, gripping the saddle's pommel. The horse was a little under sixty feet away from Fenn when she began whinnying miserably, as if she was in pain. Fenn put his arms up in the air, palms outwards like he'd once seen Halflin do to slow a wild horse that had been mauled by a wolf. That horse had galloped, bleeding and wild-eyed along the jetty to the Punchlock, rearing to jump in where it would have surely been drowned, but Halflin had stood his ground. This horse reared up on her hind legs in the same way, her eyes flickering in terror. She bucked again, more aggressively this time, as if determined to throw the rider off her back.

"Steady girl!" Fenn hushed. "Steady!"

He took a single solid pace towards her and reached his hands up higher, patting the air down. She bucked again, but this time Fenn realised the rider didn't have her reins at all, and they were flapping loose. He snatched them, winding them around his bunched fist and pulling them taut. The leather was soaked through and the horse was also drenched. She shied again, more half-heartedly now and the rider slumped drunkenly to one side. His clothes were sopping wet too and his black hair had been unbraided and clung to his handsome face. It was Gerran.

"Whoa!" Fenn cried. He put his hand on the horse's hot neck again. "Gerran?" he asked, bewildered.

Gerran wasn't clinging to the saddle at all; his wrists had been strapped to the pommel and his feet were lashed into the stirrups to fix him to his mount. Fenn gently touched his shoulder and he slid sideways, water trickling from his mouth. He stared at Fenn with open but unseeing eyes. A crude yellow scythe had been painted across his face. A Sunkmark.

Amber screamed, over and over again, clapping her hands over her face in horror. Fathom dragged her away, holding her tight, while Fenn stared in dismay down the misty causeway.

"This is what Scratch was trying to say – they're coming!"

The guards carried Gerran's body back to Moray while the children ran on ahead. As soon as they got through the main gates, Fenn, Amber and Fathom raced back to Gulper and Comfort, but by the time they burst in, news of Gerran's death had already reached them. Gulper was bundling Comfort up into her coat, his fingers trembling, and her bag was stuffed full with anything they could possibly need. He'd spent so long on the Shanties, fighting to live, that he seemed to have a nose for danger and had smelt it long before he knew exactly what the danger was.

"Is it true?" Gulper asked, his face pale and worn out with the twitches of old.

Fenn nodded grimly. "Stay here!" he ordered them, "I'm going to find Moray!"

His eye fell on Comfort, cuddling Tikki, shivering with fear, and his voice faded as he lost his nerve. Suddenly seeing little Comfort made him think it was ridiculous to think they could fight the Terras; they wouldn't stand a chance. Even if Chilstone were killed, there were enough Terras on the marsh to crush the Sargassons for ever. If the Terras attacked tonight, they'd all be done for; there wasn't time to set their plan in motion. Fenn cursed himself for bringing yet more trouble on the Sargassons.

Haven't they suffered enough? Lundy had once said.

All for Fenn. It was always for him. The name Fenn Demari was a curse.

He sped down the walkway to the great sequoia. The guards were already climbing up into the trees to start banging on the iron drums to sound the alarm. Mothers called their children in and barred their doors. People ran by in panic. By the time Fenn reached the fortress, dozens of people were streaming towards it too, trying to find out if the rumours were true. Fenn squeezed past them, unable to answer their desperate questions. He scrambled up the last steps and went inside. The guards slammed the door shut after him.

Gerran had been laid on the same truckle bed Fenn had rested in after he'd collapsed from exhaustion. Moray knelt in the salt water pooling on the floor, tenderly stroking his brother's wet hair, his shoulders shaking with silent grief and rage. At twenty-eight, Gerran was ten years younger than Moray, but now he looked like he hadn't left his teens. Someone had closed his eyes so he looked as if he was just sleeping; death had cleared all signs of age and his face shone in the dark room. The yellow paint had been wiped away, all except a small smudge missed on his chin, as if buttercup-shine had settled there permanently.

Mattie, the woman who had stitched up Fenn, stood in the corner, her shoulders shuddering as she clutched her apron to her face to stifle her weeping. She had nursed Moray and his brother as children after their mother died. In her hand Fenn saw she carried a rag, stained yellow from the Sunkmark. Young guards stood mutely nearby, their eyes wide with fear and their mouths set grim with anger. They had been just five years old when Chilstone last visited the Sargassons, but old enough to remember.

"Drowned!" Moray whispered as Fenn stumbled through the room to him. "They drowned him!"

His shoulders shook with silent grief and rage. He staggered to his feet, staring at Fenn blackly, his pale face whiter than ever and crumpled with pain.

"Chilstone sent a message." It was only then that Fenn's eyes fell on the scrap of damp paper Moray clutched in his fist. "He wants me to hand you over," Moray said, his voice cracking. "By midnight."

Fenn gritted his teeth. What was it hideous old Nile

had said? *Be careful what you wish for.* He was right after all: dreams of Resistance and revenge seemed to have brought only unhappiness. Fenn stared at poor Gerran. In the little time he'd known him, Gerran had shown him kindness. Now he was dead because of him. If Fenn hadn't ended up on the Shanties the people there could have carried on living in peace – perhaps Chilstone would even have spared Halflin. Fenn had to put a stop to it all and do the right thing; no more running, no more hiding. He made up his mind; he would give himself up. Now that he thought of it, he wondered why he hadn't done it earlier. He was what Chilstone wanted. He put his hand on Moray's shoulder.

"I brought this on you," Fenn whispered, his voice hoarse with guilt.

Moray shook his head.

"You're wrong. The Terras would have come sooner or later. The forest is too valuable for them to ignore."

"But if I give myself up, I could buy you more time," Fenn said. He felt ready; he just had to be sure his friends would be OK. "But first I want to say goodbye to my friends. And promise me you'll make sure they're all right!" His voice rasped and tears stung in his eyes.

"Only you can do that," Moray said stubbornly, shaking his head. "Chilstone stole our hopes once. Never again. I'll never give the Demari family up. Maya was my friend, friends look after each other, and each other's children. You have to get to safety."

Fenn shook his head; there was no way he was leaving the Sargassons to fight alone.

"If I'm not handing myself in, then I'll stay to fight!" he said. "I'm not running away!"

"It's not the time to fight. We're not ready!" Moray answered, his eyes blazing. "Without the prisoners on the Hellhulks there are too few of us."

"At least give me one of your guns. Let me back on the marsh ... I could kill him!" Fenn begged. His heart was set on revenge, not hiding. "Chilstone killed my grandad!"

"And my brother," Moray said quietly. "Every single one of us has a reason to want Chilstone dead. The Seaborn that kills him, kills him for us all. But for now we'll dig in – use the water against them. The Swampscrews are for marsh only. Nothing heavier than a horse can cross the causeway, and the river is too deep for the Swampscrews. Even if they get into the forest, we know it better than Terras."

Moray clapped his hand on Fenn's shoulder.

"Leave Chilstone to me. Your job is to get word to the other tribes to help us. The Sargassons can't stand alone, not again. That is the best thing you can do to help."

"But how?" asked Fenn. "Where do I go?"

"Get across the Valence Channel to the Mainland. The

Sargassons have friends in the islands off its western coast. Find them. Tell them the Sargassons of East Marsh are besieged and call on them to help. I've already sent word to the Hellhulks. Thousands of our people are there; if they can break free, they'll fight too." Moray opened a chest on the table and pulled out a map and a compass. "But first you have to get off the marsh." He opened the map and pointed at the river that snaked through Sargasson territories. The map had the same landmarks as Halflin's, but showed a multitude of new rivers. The rising water was forcing its way through the last of the marshlands.

"See here ... a tributary runs through the forest before it rejoins the main river. We'll give you and your friends boats. Travel downriver another mile to where the water narrows; soon after you'll see an old oak with a lightning strike in its crown."

At this Moray grabbed Fenn by the shoulders to make sure he'd taken it in.

"Remember; an oak with a lightning strike in its crown. You must get off the river there on the left bank! Terras from the Hellhulks regularly patrol that stretch of river. Scuttle the coracles. Go five miles south until you see a stone bridge on the right. Beyond that there's a wreck, hiding a mooring place. There's a ferryman called Lodka – a Landborn, but he's a friend. Tell him I sent you – he'll get you off East

Marsh. After that, you and your friends are on your own."

He nodded at the nearest guard who gripped Fenn's arm. "Take him out by the eel bucks," he said. As the guard stepped forward, Moray suddenly grabbed Fenn and pulled him close, wrapping his arms around him. "Keep yourself safe! You are the only Demari left. Our only hope," he whispered in Fenn's ear. "You are my family now. Go out; spread the word that the Sargassons are no longer hiding. Tell every Seaborn we fight for Fenn Demari."

13

By the time Fenn arrived on the banks of the tributary, his friends were already huddled together, shivering in the night air. The river glugged slowly past, black as tar beneath the trees. Tikki instantly jumped down from Comfort's arms and scampered up into Fenn's, squeaking with delight.

Sargasson guards had dragged two coracles through the reeds to the shoreline. The boats were like huge half walnut shells, almost circular, with a broad seat spanning across the centre. They were woven from willow, covered in tarred leather, and two short-handled paddles stained by the eel blood pooling in their base. Fenn had sometimes seen Sargassons use the coracles for travelling across the marsh, where they skimmed over the waterways to collect the eels from the eel bucks. They could be used in water from a few inches to many feet deep and they were light enough to carry on the back when the water got too shallow. They would be perfect for crossing the waterlogged marshlands. As Magpie had warned him, the waters were on the rise again.

Fenn climbed in one coracle with Gulper, while Amber and Fathom took Comfort in theirs. Tikki curled tight around Fenn's neck and chattered; he didn't like the smell of blood and sensed danger. Fenn opened up his rucksack and gently lowered him inside.

"Quiet," he whispered. Tikki twitched his nose, and curled in a ball inside.

"Tell the world the Sargassons need help. Good luck!" the guard said as he pushed Fenn and Gulper's coracle out into the creek. Amber, Fathom and Comfort weren't far behind. The current was strong and soon the two coracles were speeding downriver. Apart from the odd croaks of the natterjack toads and flurries of snowflakes hitting the water like waves breaking, the night was still.

"Could we go all the way to the sea in these things?" Fathom asked.

Fenn put his fingers to his lips. Sounds had a knack of carrying on the night air.

They slid in silence through the gloomy forest, only paddling when they had to get around dead trees floating in the water. Bogbean and spearwort grew in tangled clumps along the edge of the banks, like the dark shapes that lurked on the edge of all their nightmares. Whenever the water got too clogged with weed, Fenn showed them how to use their paddles as punts. The night crept damply on and finally even the toads fell quiet.

It was hours before they eventually reached the outer edge of the petrified forest. They were already numb with cold, and without the protection of the trees, a bleak wind blew in from the east, fattening the sides of the dwindling trees with fleeces of dusty snow. It seemed like they had been paddling for ever. Fenn scanned the riverbanks for the oak tree Moray had told him to look for. He couldn't see it but he was sure it had to be soon.

"Keep to the left," Fenn whispered, gesturing to the other bank. They paddled to the sides, hugging the bank and slowing the coracles. Suddenly a moorhen scuttled across the water's surface towards them, making them all jump. Something downriver must have spooked her. Fenn signalled to Fathom to row the coracles into the dark reeds. Under their cover, Fenn raised himself up and peered downriver.

It was dead quiet ahead and the snow clouds filled the night sky but Fenn could see how a little further ahead the river narrowed just as Moray had said it would. But there was something else; Fenn's sharp eyes spotted a darker patch between the two banks ahead. Something was lying across the water from bank to bank.

"What is it?" whimpered Gulper fearfully. But before Fenn could reply, a blistering beam of white light shot out from a huge searchlight, illuminating it properly. It was a temporary pontoon bridge – rolled planks floating on barrels in the water. It gently bobbed up and down as the river's currents changed tempo. Terra guards were already stationed on it. Fenn quickly ducked down.

"Terras!" he whispered. "The attack must have started!"

Gulper clamped his arms around himself the way he did when he was really scared.

"What're we going to do?" Amber asked.

"We've got to get out of the water right now. Dump the coracles!" Fenn answered, but at that moment Fathom silently pointed down the bank; lights were moving up the side of the river heading in their direction. Fathom peered over the edge of the coracle.

"Can we swim for it?"

"They'll see us." Gulper blinked fearfully. Comfort pressed even closer to Amber.

"Not if we're under the water," Fenn said.

"Underwater?" Amber hissed incredulously. "None of us can stay under as long as you. We're not built like you Fenn! We're not half fish!"

Fenn fell silent, trying to think over Amber's panic but she continued, shaking her head at the very idea of swimming.

"You can make it. You go! It'd be better for us if you did."

Gulper blinked anxiously at Fenn, willing him to have an answer. He started rocking again to calm himself down, making the coracle shake.

"I'm not leaving you," Fenn said firmly, holding Gulper's shoulder tight to still him.

He desperately tried to think of some plan to save them, but couldn't find any answer. They couldn't retreat; there was no way they'd have the strength to paddle back up the river – the current was too strong and the river too wide to cross back to the forest without being spotted. He turned and looked at Fathom to see if he could think of something. Fathom had survived the Shanties for a long time; surely together they could work out a way. Fathom silently shook his head.

"Can't we just hide?" Amber asked. "In the reeds?" But even she knew that was ridiculous. She looked imploringly at Fenn to come up with something.

"Maybe it's time to give up?" Fathom said quietly.

Fenn refused to do that, however impossible it seemed. There always had to be a way; Halflin would never have given up. His eyes alighted on the bulrushes; tall as bamboo, white as milk, straight as wands. He suddenly remembered a story Halflin had once told him about a prank he'd once played on a childhood friend. Fenn had the answer. He quickly slid his knife out and sliced four reeds down. They couldn't hide in the reeds but the reeds could hide them.

"What the hell are you doing?" Amber hissed. "What are we going to do with those?"

"You can breathe through them!" said Fenn. His friends still looked at him blankly. "You *can* stay under if you breathe through them," he explained. "Go with the current, try not to kick. Don't break the surface."

"What about the bridge?" Amber cut in immediately. "How do we get past that? It's floating on the actual water – the reeds won't help us then!"

"Leave it to me, all right?" Fenn whispered. "Just make sure you get in the water when the Terras get close. Once you see me go under, give me ten minutes. Then follow."

"Even if we get down the river, what about when we get out? We'll freeze!" Gulper asked, already shivering pitifully.

Fenn was already stripping off the top layers of his clothes and flattening them down in the bottom of the coracle.

"Put them in here. They're not going to waste time stopping an empty boat," he said, nodding to them to put their clothes with his.

They all knew it was a crazy plan but they had no other choice. Amber quickly unbuttoned her coat, helped Comfort pull off her outer layers, and pressed them deep in the bottom of the coracle, covering them with deerskins. Comfort lifted Tikki up to Fenn questioningly. Fenn took him and stared hard into his eyes.

"You've got to go on your own, Tikki," he whispered, sounding as firm as possible. "You've got to run that way!" Fenn pointed downstream, then kissed him on the head and gently gave him a nudge into the watery reeds.

Mongeese can swim, but Tikki didn't want to; and for a second he tried to wriggle out of Fenn's hands and back into the coracle, looking over his shoulder at Fenn with large puzzled eyes.

"Yes, you've got to go," Fenn said. "That way!"

He nodded in the direction he wanted Tikki to take, and this time Tikki seemed to understand and slid into the water towards the bank.

Fenn turned to the others. "When you get past the bridge, we'll meet by the lightning tree."

"What are you going to do?" Fathom asked.

"Cut the bridge in half," Fenn explained.

"What?" Amber said. "Have you gone completely out of your mind? That's your plan?"

"It's just barrels held together with ropes – how hard can it be?"

Fenn edged his leg over the coracle's side and climbed

into the water; it was so cold he felt like his skin was peeling off. His whole body stippled with goose pimples and he shuddered as the icy cold stabbed his muscles.

"Ten minutes," he reminded Amber. His teeth were already chattering until he clamped his knife between them.

"Be careful," Amber whispered.

Fenn swam out into the centre of the river, taking a sharp breath as the cold slammed around his heart. There, he turned and gave his friends the thumbs up, before sliding under, out of sight.

He felt like his bones would snap, it was so freezing, but at least there was light from the Terras' searchlight so that he could see the muddy landscape he was swimming through. Knobbly branches of dead trees stuck up like birds' claws and small fish glimmered as they flittered past in the murky weeds. Deep below he could just make out the shapes of thick, black eels squirming in the mud.

Fenn swam underwater for more than two minutes, with the current speeding him along until he reached the bridge. Then he dived deeper to duck beneath the rows of barrels and came up the other side, behind the Terras, who were still patrolling back and forth – keeping watch upriver, not down. He waited for the nearest Terra guard to pass, then grabbed the first rope linking two central barrels in the chain holding the bridge together. The rope was the thickness of his arm and would take a lot of work to cut through with his little knife, blunted through weeks of use at the Shanties. He sawed as quickly and quietly as he could before the Terra guard passed back again. He was almost through the first rope when suddenly the bridge began to bounce up and down violently.

An entire unit of Terras were tramping across. Fenn ducked down under the water again and waited for the men to cross. Finally the unit crossed, leaving just the Terra guards. Fenn resurfaced and made the last cuts before the strands fretted to nothing.

Fenn dived under the bridge to find the second rope. This one was going to be much harder; he'd have to stay underwater or else he'd be spotted. His legs were starting to cramp and he was losing feeling in his fingers, but his friends were depending on him and the ten minutes would soon be up. He felt light-headed, and his skin felt water-logged. He was exhausted but he couldn't stop. He started hacking at the second rope. It was difficult underwater, but with the last of his strength he finally managed to cut through.

He felt like his lungs were going to split open, and with the last of his breath he swam back towards the bank. His head broke the surface of the river, amongst the reeds, coughing out mouthfuls of water before gulping down the wonderful, sweet fresh air, feeling as though he had never breathed properly before. Dizzy and weak, he looked back at the pontoon bridge, waiting for something to happen. But nothing did. His heart was in his mouth; his friends must be close to it now.

Just as he thought all his work had been for nothing, there came a grinding sound; and the two central barrels began to separate. As the river surged through, the gap widened and each side of the bridge swept back hard towards the banks. The bridge started disintegrating and the air filled with howls from the Terras losing their balance, dropping to their hands and knees as they tried to stay aboard, clinging on to the barrels like rats on a sinking ship.

Fenn waded through the reeds and up onto the bank. Keeping to the shadows, he ran bent-backed along the edge of the river, scanning for the tree he'd told the others to meet him at. After a few minutes' running he spotted an oak tree with dark, twisted branches and guessed it was the one Moray had meant. He flopped down in its shadow, watching the river carefully for signs of his friends. The coracle spun into view first. Fenn lunged back into the water and hauled it up onto the bank and under the tree. He rummaged under the deerskins and pulled out his dry clothes, scrambling into them before bundling his wet things into one of the skins and knotting it.

Once he was dry, he let out a low whistle, peering into the blackness around him to catch a glimpse of Tikki. At last he spotted a movement in sedge grass that grew between the river and the tree. He whistled again and the grass trembled once more. He crawled over and fished down into the wet fronds. It was Tikki.

"Good boy!" he whispered, picking him up and giving him a squeeze. He rubbed him dry with his own jumper, then pushed Tikki down under his shirt to get him warm, tucking in the shirt to make a sort of bag. He ran back to the shadows of the tree, beating his arms around himself to try to get his circulation going. He was so cold that the blood rang in his ears and he didn't immediately hear the rustling in the reeds as Fathom appeared, pulling Amber up onto the bank. Gulper had Comfort on his back; she had her eyes shut and her teeth were clattering so much that Fenn could hear them from ten paces. He scrambled over to them, pulling them one by one up onto the bank, and they changed into their dry things underneath the scorched boughs of the old oak.

"You're the craziest person I've ever met," Fathom said.

"*Any of us* have ever met," Amber corrected him, rubbing Comfort's hair dry.

"Crazy or not, it worked, didn't it?" Gulper said protectively. "We got out!"

But they weren't out of the woods yet; Fenn glanced

anxiously at the lightening sky; only a few stars remained and it would be dawn soon.

"We've got to get on that ferry tonight," he said, "or else find somewhere to hide." Fenn sliced his knife through the coracle to sink it, and they headed off along the riverside, keeping their eyes open for the bridge. They had been running for more than half an hour, when Fenn stopped to scan the marsh, hoping to see the bridge. But he couldn't get any sense of the geography; nothing seemed to be as Moray had described.

Instead he saw something grey sticking up in the distance; an old concrete pipe, the type once laid in the futile effort to drain the ever-increasing water. It must have been pushed up during one of the Risings and now poked up, its end gaping like a cave.

"In there," he ordered. "It's getting too light to be out."

Birds were starting to sing as they raced across the frost-white marsh and scrambled in. The pipe was at least ten feet wide, and there was plenty of room for all of them. Dry leaves had blown in and as the children huddled down, Amber quickly scooped them around them all, like a nest, to keep them warm.

Once they had caught their breath, Fenn pulled out Moray's map, trying to work out where they were, while Amber wrapped one of the furs around Comfort's shoulders, rubbing them briskly, and laid another over Gulper. Exhausted, and in shock, Comfort laid her head in Amber's lap and Amber started softly crooning an old song while stroking her hair.

It was a tune she'd remembered the evening before as she was falling asleep, something she thought her mother must have sung once. She'd managed to recall the tune well: a lilting melody that sounded sad, but the few words she remembered made no sense. She'd only managed to dredge up odd snippets, so that mid-humming she'd suddenly sing random phrases. It lifted her heart to have retrieved them, like finding something precious you'd thought you'd lost for ever in the sand.

"*Hm, hmhm, hmhm, hm,* cat and the fiddle, *hm, hmm, hm, hm-m,* the moon, the little dog laugh'd *hm hm-m hm hm, hm hm hm* ran away with the spoon."

Amber stroked Comfort's hair slower as her eyes began to blink heavily. Even though they were in terrible danger, Comfort felt safe nuzzled against Amber, the heat of her voice batting the top of her head as she began another song. Hearing the soft singing, Tikki at last dared to peep out of Fenn's shirt, but was now so warm he decided he'd stay there. Amber had to whistle to him to coax him from his little nest and into Comfort's lap. At last he ventured out and nuzzled against Comfort's cheek, making her giggle.

He settled in her lap for a long sleep and began to purr.

"I think we're here..." Fenn said to Fathom, but before Fathom could look, Gulper broke in.

"When are we ever going to stop running?" he asked, closing his eyes as he rested his head on Amber's shoulder. "I was better off on the Shanties."

Amber jerked her shoulder to shove him off. "Don't you ever let me hear you say that again! Not ever!" she hissed in an angry whisper so as not to wake Comfort. "We're free! We were never free there. Being free's everything!"

But their freedom was coming to an end. Without having heard a thing, the pipe suddenly flooded with a hot, white light, blinding them. It flashed into the corners at the end, making a water rat they hadn't spied scurry back into its hole.

"Got ourselves a decent haul here!" a voice boomed.

14

It was clear to Fenn that the Terras didn't know who they'd caught. They were just lowly wardens from the Hellhulks on a standard patrol, picking up any and every stray Seaborn on the run.

Even if they had been given direct orders to hunt for Fenn Demari, they would never have recognised him; his eye was still bloated and bloodshot, making it difficult to distinguish any colour at all. He was also wearing Sargasson clothes of eel-skin and rabbit furs, and his hair was still sewn in braids.

The Terras pushed them up a track that ran through deep reeds bent heavy with snow. A battered old truck was already waiting and they were shoved aboard as the canvas roof was pinned down around them. Two teenage boys, ragged and rake-thin were already huddled inside, their arms around each other, shivering with the cold. Two of the Terras climbed up at the back to make sure none of them tried to jump out as it bumped along a rough track running alongside the winding river.

"Where are you taking us?" Fathom asked the Terra guarding them, a weasel-faced man with a scraggy moustache covering a narrow, mean mouth.

"You're honoured; you're going to join the greatest labour force ever," he sneered. His clothes were soaked through and his jowls hung tired and burnt red with the cold, like a chicken's wattle. He wiped his nose on his sleeve, leaving a snail-slick. "After we've caught our quota," he added morosely. Fenn realised he was talking about Seaborns. Once the truck was packed, the Terras got their rations; food was getting so scarce that only Chilstone's elite guards got full supplies. Fenn made sure he was by Comfort's side so he could slip Tikki out of her arms and hide him back under his shirt. It had crossed his mind to try and drive Tikki away onto the marsh, but Tikki was too tame now and would certainly have been caught by a wolf within hours, or, judging by the hunger-hollowed eyes of the guards, they would have happily turned him into a meal too.

The only time the children saw daylight was when the Terras opened the tarpaulin to jump out, looking for more stray Seaborns taking shelter in a shipwreck or in the roof space of a submerged house. From out of the eaves of a derelict windmill they winkled out one ancient old man – so shortsighted that he had to grope his way up onto the truck – and a woman hiding with him, who seemed to be his daughter, judging from the way she fretted over him. They looked Scotian with their flame-coloured hair, but neither of them spoke English, or else they were too afraid to talk, and they stared at the children dumbfounded. When the guard wasn't looking, Fenn managed to snatch a glimpse through a chink in the canvas to try and work out where they were, but the snow made everything look the same under the endless vaulted white skies.

The children huddled together with Comfort squished down between them. Gulper was rocking unhappily, clutching his bony knees like he always did when he was at his most scared. Fathom tried patting his back, but he was in a daze of terror.

Amber nudged Gulper roughly in the ribs. "Hey, remember that thumb thing we used to do, Gulper? How'd we do it? I want to show Comfort," she said.

Gulper shrugged indifferently, glazed and blank.

"C'mon!" she whispered in his ear. "For Comfort's sake. She's really scared."

Gulper peered at Comfort and mustered all he had to

shoulder away his fear and whispered, "Ever done Thumb Wars, Comfort?"

Comfort's lips were clamped tight together to stop herself from crying and she shook her head miserably. Gulper swapped places with Amber and gripped Comfort's hand.

"Well, you haven't lived! Wanna play?"

He grabbed her hand, and locked their two thumbs together, his ugly bitten stub against hers – tiny, neat and somehow immaculate despite all they'd been through.

"Be gentle!" he pleaded. He made a show of gulping hard, as if he was afraid of Comfort's strength. "Right, let's do it. One, two, three, four, I declare a thumb war!"

They wrestled their thumbs together, each time Gulper conceding to Comfort's superior strength, sometimes putting up more of a fight to make her triumph sweeter. The two of them played through their fears while the other Seaborns looked on, even managing to smile a few times as they watched.

It was early evening by the time the truck rattled over a wide bridge and jolted to a rough halt, making everyone fall forwards. Fenn slid his hand beneath his shirt, and gave Tikki a tickle to show him everything was all right. For the next half an hour, they waited in the freezing cold. From the other side of the canvas, the air rang with an ugly orchestra of iron on stone: the brittle clatter of rock being hammered. Occasionally there came a dull boom of explosives in the distance. There was a constant chugging sound, and the relentless grind of engines and heavy machinery under strain. Suddenly a Terra slammed down the ramp at the back of the truck.

"Welcome to your new home!" he shouted, giving Fenn a hard clap on the shoulders and pushing him and the other children out. They shuffled forwards with the others, stumbling down the ramp, blinking into a bleak, white light. Fenn immediately grabbed hold of Amber and Comfort's hands and pulled them closer. He knew they had to stick together – their lives might depend on it.

"You two!" he hissed to Gulper and Fathom, who had fallen behind a few paces. "Get over here!"

They were in a stony, pock-marked field less than a mile from the Wall. It looked like a reflection of the ocean it flanked; vast and grey. It was the first time Fenn had seen the Wall up close and he got a crick in his neck from looking up at the top of it, while its sheer height made him feel giddy. Around them were piles of rocks and raggedy children sat cross-legged, grading the stones according to their size, while women broke up larger boulders using massive lump hammers with handles taller than themselves.

It was a pitiful sight and the children winced to see how exhausted and scrawny they looked. In the entire compound, there wasn't one spark of joy. The Shanties had been tough and rough, but even there friendships and loyalties sprang up between people; families stuck together. Here, men silently pulled sledges laden with rocks towards a wide canal, and five huge river barges were being loaded with the heavy blocks of stone. A team of stocky-legged cobs whinnied unhappily as they were harnessed to the barges to pull them through the wetlands to the Wall, where buttresses were being built to strengthen it. Through all of this, a set of rails ran down into a trough before entering an enormous black hole. The other end of the tracks led onto the shore where they met a pontoon bridge built from huge split tree trunks suspended on thick chains. The bridge led out to sea, rising and falling with the tides.

Now the sea mists were clearing as the day warmed up the children could see the outline of two huge Hellhulks, anchored out at sea. One had listed so violently to one side that its rudder was visible above the chopping waves. This was the *Hercules*, one of the first Fearzeros decommissioned by the Terra Firma when she ran aground and was turned into a prison. She was the first Hellhulk to take the place of the old Terra Firma Missions; Chilstone saw no point in taking up space on the land if Seaborns could be housed at sea, where they belonged. The *Hercules* had never been made secure and after years of heavy rains, she had keeled over, drowning the inmates whose prison-brigs were port-side. Now deserted, hundreds of gulls screeched and flapped around the gaping holes left on her deck where her gun turrets had been ripped out, and the ship was white with their droppings.

The other ship, the *Brimstone,* was blackened with grime and oil, only upright with the aid of enormous props: the trunks of firs harvested from the edges of the Sargassons' forest. The ship was practically unrecognisable as a Fearzero now. The *Brimstone* had been stripped of its gun turrets too, and the gaps plugged with enormous chimneys belching smoke over the sky in thick brown clots. The hull was hidden beneath dozens of shacks, scabbing the ship's sides like a canker. The little that could be seen of its iron hull revealed splits between the huge metal sheets where the rivets had rusted away so the twinkling of lights and fires inside were visible.

Where the bridge reached the ship's side, it broadened into a wide platform on which stood four Terras in front of a giant drawbridge hacked into the Hellhulk. As Fenn watched, they shunted back the huge metal bolts securing the drawbridge, before cranking the iron handles either side. With its rusty chains groaning, the drawbridge slowly creaked down onto the pontoon and a horde of ragtag men, women and children were driven out from the bowels of the ship, down onto the bridge and back over to the shore. The *Brimstone* made Fenn think of something greedy; a gaping mouth with a tongue rolled out, bursting at the seams from gorging.

"Wait here!" the Terra shouted at them as soon as the last labourers disappeared into the deep wound of the mine. A whistle sounded and the labour force that had been waiting underground appeared on their way back to the Hellhulk, pushed into line by the Terra Trusties; prisoners who got special privileges for helping the Terras keep control.

If the people going into the mine looked in a sorry state, it was nothing to how those coming out looked. Shambling along the bridge, they clumped together, not bumping or jostling each other, too exhausted for even that. They looked as if they had come from a wet fire; their skin was boiled red and their clothes were drenched. As soon as the last of them had stepped onto the bridge, the Trusties pushed the children into the crowds.

"Stay tight together!" Fenn whispered. "We have to stay together!" He pulled Amber and Comfort even closer, and Fathom and Gulper bundled in behind as they began to edge towards the *Brimstone*.

Seawater washed over their feet as the bridge bounced under the weight of so many. Green slime coated the wood, making it hard to stand up without slipping and

Fenn suddenly lost his footing. Instantly he felt his hand being grabbed as he slid away towards the choppy waves. For a brief, happy second he was reminded of Halflin; a hand reaching down to him with the same gnarled and calloused skin, the same firm grip. Fenn's heart skipped a beat, but instead of Halflin's face he found himself looking into the eyes of a decrepit old man, his face brown and wrinkled as a crumpled-up bag. Watery eyes stared intently into his.

"I'm Humber," he smiled as he helped steady him.

He was bow-legged and scrawny as a rook. When he swallowed, his Adam's apple jumped in his throat like a frog in a bag. From his heavy-lidded eyes and pepper-black hair Fenn guessed he was Venetian, but having seen how a new set of clothes had turned himself into a Sargasson in so many people's eyes, he knew such guesses were pointless. Seaborns were all have-nots – that was their distinct mark. It had been petty differences of hair and skin colour that made them fight each other instead of Terras, and even a true Seaborn, as Fenn was supposed to be, could easily have their webbed toes cut. Even so, it was too early to know if Humber could be trusted.

Seeing the suspicion in Fenn's eyes, Humber shrugged sadly. "You'll have to trust someone in here to survive," he said, staring ahead as if he was thinking aloud. "You're all new, aren't you?" he asked, glancing at the children. Fenn nodded hesitantly.

"Listen to me. If you don't trust anyone, you've got no one to watch your back. Like him." He looked at the man in front of him as they tramped back towards the ship. Fenn followed his gaze. The woman walking by his side was one of the newly caught Seaborns. She was pale and pinched, and probably hadn't eaten for a week. She slipped her hand in the man's pocket and pulled out a mouldy piece of rice bread, before tucking it back in her own.

"And she doesn't trust anyone either," Humber said, as the bread slipped from her pocket into the mouth of a little boy standing just waist-high. "And so it goes on. And on. Seaborn pitted against Seaborn." He shook his head sadly, but slipped a wink at the child. "Safest place in your tummy, eh? Clever fella," he said.

Humber leant in towards Amber and Fenn as they shuffled on up the bridge towards the Hellhulk. "Keep tight hold of each other when you get inside. They'll try to separate you. Thick as thieves, remember." He wagged his finger at them. "Come and find me. Deck Three."

Fenn nodded. Some instinct in him told him Humber could be trusted, and Halflin had always told him to trust instinct above all else. He grabbed hold of Amber's coat and pulled Comfort so she was directly between them, but

Gulper and Fathom were already being pushed over to the other side of the bridge by people surging between them, struck by the force of Terras shoving up from behind. Fenn managed to grab the collar of Gulper's jacket and yanked them both back towards him.

They had reached the end of the bridge under the shadow of the ship's prow, soaring over them like a rusty old axe. Gulls screeched in the air and the wind rattled the loose sheets of steel, so the whole ship clanked and grumbled like a failing machine. They were far enough out at sea for the water to be getting rough, and waves slapped up in the gap between the end of the bridge and the drawbridge. Amber and Fenn jumped across, keeping hold of Comfort, but when they landed on the other side, they realised that Fathom and Gulper had got separated from them again.

They were in the bowels of the ship, a huge room, its cavernous ceiling encrusted with rusting pipework that wormed its way around the sides of the rotting hull. Odd chinks of light crept in from the splitting sheets of iron that clad the ship, and from the tiny oil lamps fixed to the bulkheads, but it was gloomy with smoke. Crumbling iron ladders led up to the higher decks, with steel-grilled walkways braced between. Wherever there were junctions or ledges – under ladders or between the bulkheads – people had made themselves tiny living areas where they had to sleep. There were at least a thousand people in this room alone, with more trudging down from the upper decks to collect their rations. Amber and Fenn held hands tightly to keep from being swept along with the crowd as the drawbridge was winched up behind them. It clunked shut and they were plunged into semi-darkness.

One of the Trusties announced over a loudspeaker that rations had arrived, and in their desire to be first, more and more prisoners surged from behind. Fenn grabbed hold of Comfort and Amber's hands even more tightly. He looked around, searching the crowds for Humber, but like Fathom and Gulper, he too had disappeared. Ahead, there were rails, like cattle stalls, where two brutish Trusties were forcing people into separate compartments. The sudden influx meant there was a bottleneck and no one was moving properly any more.

There was a sudden commotion as a man started roaring at one of the Trusties, as he tried to drag his child away from him. The child was screaming too. He was large and burly, with fists as big as mallets, but the Trusty didn't hesitate to pull out a truncheon and start beating him. He blew his whistle and Terra guards ran over. Within seconds they swamped the man and dragged him away. There were at least thirty prisoners to one Trusty, but no one turned to help the man and his child. The Trusties could be even more vicious than the Terras and no one wanted to make a move that could hurt them, or someone they loved. Humber suddenly reappeared by Fenn's shoulder.

"I thought I told you lot to stick together?" he hissed angrily, herding them towards the bulkhead. "C'mon, keep close!"

They pushed through the last few people and found themselves by a rickety steel ladder that ran up one of the walls. They clambered up and saw a second stairway that led upwards again. They scrambled up that one too, scratching their shins on the jagged edges of missing rungs, but before they reached the top, Humber leant down and yanked each of them through. Fathom and Gulper were already waiting.

"Always stick together!" Humber said. "Rule number one!" Before Fenn could reply, he'd turned his back on them. "This way," he said over his shoulder.

Humber pushed aside a rough cloth and they found themselves on the mid-deck of the Hellhulk, in a wide cabin spanning a quarter of the Hellhulk's length.

"The kitchens – the best deck," Humber explained. Gulper nodded in agreement. "Got a bit of air in here, but not too cold." He gestured to a giant chimney made from old corrugated pipe, which nearly filled the opening left by the removal of the gun turret and pierced through the floor of the next deck. "Up there blows daggers for draughts."

All around the bulkheads and off the deck beams, old sacks and nets hung like spiders' webs in which people were already trying to sleep in them. In the centre of the deck, others huddled for warmth around the chimney, which had several holes hacked out; so there were at least three separate fireplaces in which to cook. Strips of firelight spoked out from these, as bright as sunbeams. Several women stood with their backs to them, working together to cook in large iron pots hanging from bars directly over the flames. Aged men and women bundled in old rags, squatted on two huge oak sleepers flanking the stove, like a shelf of long-forgotten washing. They were huddled together and drinking from tin mugs, making steam billow around their heads. Toddlers and young children played games with stones and chalk at their feet. Around each child's neck dangled a spoon with a hole punched through the stem, threaded on a piece of string or leather lace.

"See them?" Humber asked, pointing at the spoons. "Get yourselves one of those ... or a mug, or you won't get nothin' from the pots." He cast an eye over them. "I'll sort something out," he said kindly. One of the women lifted a cauldron out of the fire and called the children from their playing. They rushed over, dipping their spoons straight in, before scrapping with each other for bigger portions.

"We try to get the kids and the olds fed first," Humber explained as he pushed them towards the fire.

The old men and women nudged and elbowed each other along irritably, grumbling at the interruption, but eventually they budged up enough for the children to squash in. Immediately their clothes began to steam as they dried. A scraggy little boy wearing a tunic, which looked as if it had been made out of stitched blankets, handed Humber a mug of soup from the pot. But instead of drinking it, Humber passed it straight to Gulper. Gulper didn't wait to slurp it down, although before he could finish the lot, Humber prised it from his hands and passed it on to a little girl sitting by his side, looking up at them with big hungry eyes. Fenn smiled at them. Moray had got it wrong. He'd said the Seaborns were too busy fighting each other to fight the Terra Firma, but not all of them. There was still kindness if you looked for it.

"The first days will be the hardest," Humber continued. "That's when the Trusties get the sum of you. See how much they can push you around; see if you'll be trouble." He nodded surreptitiously at the Trusty that Fenn had seen beating the prisoner earlier. "But whatever you do—" he lifted a warning finger— "never, *ever* get on the wrong side of Lazlo. Mean as a snake with backache, that one. Once saw him kill a man with his bare hands … for a piece of bread smaller than this." He stuck up his thumb. He pointed to a hammock halfway along the Hellhulk's side, lying snugly in an alcove between two steel struts.

"And that's mi' kipper," he said laughing. "We're like sardines here, aren't we?" He nudged the old man next to him in the ribs who managed a puny smile. "I'll sort out a good pitch for you lot."

At this, Fathom leant close to Fenn's ear. "Why should we trust him?" he whispered, but Humber had as good a hearing as Halflin.

"No reason you should," he said pragmatically before carrying on. "Here's the deal. In the morning there'll be a roll call. Get up jack flash; they don't need an excuse to beat you, so don't give them one. Don't leave anything in your hammock; the guards steal what they can." He looked pointedly at Fenn. "And you should get that ferret out before he gives you something to remember him by."

"It's not a ferret," Fenn said, unbuttoning his shirt. "And he'd never bite me anyway." Tikki poked his head out and ran down into his lap. Immediately many little hands grabbed at him, pulling his tail and stroking him.

Humber motioned for one of the children to bring something else to eat, and the little boy dipped his mug in the soup again and brought it back for Amber first. She took a sip, blowing its warmth back up into her face and closing her eyes as she let the heat seep in. She passed the mug to Comfort.

Humber nodded at Comfort as she gulped. "Leave that little scrap with the older girl – she's too small to go down the mines. That means you three boys are going to have to work twice as hard. The more stone you dig the more grub you'll get. I'll show you what's what. There's a woman here, a cook. I'll get the girls in with her."

"Why are you helping us?" Amber asked, her face screwed up with suspicion. Humber looked at her in surprise.

"Why wouldn't I?" Humber asked. "We're all in the same boat, aren't we?"

He clapped his knees and looked around to see how many people appreciated his great wit, but even though hardly anyone had the strength to notice it, he still laughed; a rich joyful sound, deep from the centre of his scraggy body, so far down inside that meanness, cold and hunger couldn't reach it.

Fenn started laughing too, not at the joke as much as at Humber's sheer joy at having made it. As their laughter echoed across the room others turned to look and smile, or scowl, depending on how annoying they found Humber. The laugh finally reached the fireplace, causing one of the women to look up at the sound. She flipped up the rim of a black hat to hear better, and saw Fenn.

Letting out a loud whoop she hurtled towards him.

"You's like a bad penny, chil'!"

15

Magpie scooped Fenn into a tight embrace. "I don't believe it! You got off them Shanties!" Her eyes gleamed with tears of happiness, making them more buttony than ever.

"You've got a friend here already?" Humber said. "And she's a fine cook too," he added, throwing her his most charming smile.

"Tsk!" Magpie tutted, nudging Humber out of her way with her ladle. She didn't have time for his compliments; she knew he only did it to get an extra ladle of food.

"How did you end up here?" Fenn asked, as she settled down between Comfort and Amber.

"Terra Firma patrol jumped the *Panimengro* again! Course they couldn't prove Viktor done nuffin' wrong, but that didn't stop them confiscatin' his permit. Took most of the crew 'n' all! Includin' him."

At this Magpie jerked her thumb over her shoulder towards one of the Sargassons now climbing into his hammock. Fenn remembered him from when he first boarded the *Panimengro* the night he fled East Marsh; he'd been one of the musicians playing instruments made from rubbish.

"That big ol' Caspian got to go free – I bet he greased a palm – but the rest of us…" She pressed her lips together unhappily for a moment. "Like I tol' yer; my permits wouldn't fool no one."

Fenn felt terrible about Viktor. The *Panimengro*'s captain might have dumped him on the Shanties, but he had also taken a huge risk helping him get away from East Marsh.

"Where's Viktor now?" he asked.

"He's still a cap'n, but they Sunkmarked the *Panimengro*." Magpie pulled a tragic face. "Got him workin' a bone-barge now, fishin' the dead off these Hellhulks here an' dumpin' them out at sea. The same job as allus, when yer come to think on it: Viktor's allus bin carryin' Seaborn across the oceans, 'cept these ones gonna be fish-food…"

Magpie huddled in conspiratorially, drawing up her legs and resting her chin on her knees. She clicked her sharp fingers for Humber to listen up. Keeping an eye out, she grabbed Fenn's collar and jerked him nearer so she could keep her voice low. Her eyes glittered with mischief.

"I'd ask you what you've bin up to, chil', 'cept I already know," she whispered, poking him hard in the ribs and wrinkling her nose with indignation. "You think I don't know who you are? Jus' cos I don't read too good, don't you go assumifyin' I add two an' two an' make five! When them Terras came aboard, they's so interested in you I did some guessin' an' some askin' an' some workin' out myself! Them *funny* eyes, them way you knew nowt 'bout the world 'cept what you got outta books!"

Magpie leant back on her seat, casting her eye over Fenn's, and sucked her teeth.

"An' now look at you! If a Cajun cat can look at a king? An' got yourself an entourage I see!" She glared at Fenn with a mixture of infuriation and admiration. "An' they say you've been stirrin' up a whole soup of trouble! There ain't a Seaborn worth the name that don't know Fenn Demari's alive an' kickin now, thanks very much to you – an' your shenanigans!"

"So it's true?" Humber gasped, peering at Fenn with wonder. "We all heard the rumours, but we thought you were with the Marsh Sargassons. People are sayin' Moray handed you over."

"Moray would sooner die. He was the one who—" Fenn began indignantly, but before he had a chance to finish, a siren wailed.

"Curfew," Humber said. "Lazlo'll be coming." He jerked his head towards the hammocks. "Get some kip. Look smart. We'll talk more tomorrow."

Meanwhile, Magpie fished deep in her coat and pulled out a tiny black pod of vanilla, fuzzy with pocket fluff. She ripped it into minuscule pieces and handed them out to each of the children. Humber looked on hopefully, but she ignored him.

"It's my last bit. Enjoy it!" she said as she wrapped her arms around Amber and Comfort, giving them a motherly squeeze. She shot Fenn a beady look as he fed a scrap of his own bread to Tikki, still curled up in his shirt, and tutted.

"I got the sum of you when I saw you say goodbye to your granddaddy. You allus think you gotta take everythin' under your wing – but your wing ain't *big* enough for everyone. You gotta share. You gotta trust others to help."

The last lights were put out as the guards and Trusties made their final tours of the kitchens. People hurriedly made their way to their beds. Lazlo never needed an excuse to give a prisoner a beating. Humber quickly led them to an alcove, where a few empty rice sacks had been strung between the huge iron straps of the ship.

Fenn passed him his share of the vanilla pod. "Never liked the taste much," he said.

"Me neither," Humber replied, passing it back. "I'll wake you before Lazlo gets a chance to," he mumbled, climbing into his hammock. "That way you get a day gettin' used to the place before he gets you down the mine."

By sneaking the children away from the first roll call, Humber bought the boys a whole day's grace and they avoided being called for mine duty. The girls were able to stay with Magpie and the other cooks, lost in the muddle of bodies that always huddled around the stoves. But Humber couldn't hold the Trusties off for ever and when Lazlo found out what Humber had done, he docked his rations and put him on double shifts. Just as the sea was greedy for land, the Wall was hungry for stone – and the mine never seemed to stop spewing out limestone and flint.

"Ready?" Humber asked, as he hitched the leather straps from the cart over Fathom and Fenn's shoulders. Gulper was too short to be paired with anyone and was relegated to scuttling alongside, helping where he could. The boys had been put on the hardest shift as well, as punishment for their day's reprieve. With dozens of other Seaborn boys and men they rode down into the mines on the heavy oak carts. But after loading them up with the heavy limestone, the real work began in hauling them back up to the surface. Each truck was hitched to eight people to drag, but even so it was a back-breaking job, dangerous and dirty.

Humber had made sure the boys were in his team and today they were only a few hundred yards away from the strip of rock the Terras wanted mined – a seam of limestone – but it still took an hour to reach it. The tracks twisted and turned so often the cart kept derailing, and the team of workers had to lift it back on each time. When they arrived in the middle of a high cave hollowed out of the rock, they were already pouring with sweat.

The air was hot and damp in the cavern and hundreds of stalactites had formed on the rock face overhead in an arch of needles. They stopped to scoop a handful of water from one of the stone troughs around the walls, but a Trusty was soon over them, pushing them to get back to work.

"Get tooled up," Humber instructed, as they pulled the straps off their shoulders. "We'll prep this tunnel here. Wet your rags," he said, dipping his scarf in the trough. "The less dust in your pipes, the better you'll dodge sickness. Too late for some, mind." He laughed as he spat at the ground and a red stain the shape of a bursting star splodged the dust. He tied the scarf over his nose.

Leaning against the walls were iron wedges, picks and mallets. Fenn and others loaded them into rush baskets and heaved them onto their backs while Humber took a lantern from a cavity in the wall.

"Follow me," he said and led them up a short, roughly hewn slope that forked into two small caves. "If you hear a sudden ruck, it's a rockfall. Get near those." He pointed to five thick oak stanchions running up the centre of the tunnels. "They keep the roof up," he said, setting down his tools as he looked along the rock. "Won't take long; there are some natural fractures here already." He smiled encouragingly at them.

On one side of the wall a line had already been chiselled out, showing where the next blocks of limestone were to be cut.

"First things first," he said. "We need to mark the blocks out."

He hammered a guide line into the rock and tied a thin piece of rope to it, then gave the rope to Fenn, pointing to a spot further down the wall.

"Get it level with this, then we chisel. When it's deep enough, we lay the powder. The rock pops out."

Fenn pulled the rope taut and tied it to the second loop. Humber rubbed the underside of the rope with a chunk of chalk, then he held the rope out like a guitar string and let it twang back against the rock face. A white line was left and Humber tossed the chalk over to Fathom.

"Two more lines. There, and there." He pointed out

where he meant. Then turned to Gulper. "You look strong," he said unconvincingly. "Up to a bit of graft?"

Gulper nodded doubtfully. He was used to catching rats, not working with stone. He looked at the tools in his hands and felt their weight. Humber wrapped a rag around Gulper's left hand, which would hold the wedge in place.

"Work towards me, see?" he said, pointing to where the two lines would meet up. Humber then crouched down by the incisions already chopped in the rock and began to tap the iron wedge into the crevice, deepening the crack with each metallic beat. "After this we make the holes for the dynamite."

Fenn watched how Humber let the mallet bounce off the iron wedge so he'd get two or three strikes for the price of one, and copied him. It was relentless and exhausting; after an hour, the rag only stopped his skin getting broken – it didn't numb the pain of constantly striking himself.

Humber was the leader of their unit and it was his job to make sure everyone worked as hard as they could for the whole unit to earn their rations for the night. So he urged them on, and kept their spirits up, alternating between whistling, singing rude songs about Chilstone and laughing at his own jokes, which made him cough more. Now and then he'd cock his ear to the stone as if listening for an answer to a question only he knew, then he'd tell more bad jokes and tall stories – tales of shark attacks, his capture and his exploits in the Arctic when he'd been a trawler man. When he finished entertaining them with nonsense, he passed on tips about surviving in the Hellhulk, about the geology of the quarry, about the weaknesses of the Wall.

"Too rigid," he explained. "Another Rising will knock it clean off its foundations." Every now and then he'd disappear, but no one ever seemed to see where, and when he returned he was always caked with stone dust, his knuckles bleeding.

Finally the Terras sounded a siren and the workers stopped for a few minutes to take a drink. Humber had other ideas. While Fathom and Gulper huddled down, sharing a single ration of rice bread, he gave Fenn a sly nod and slipped away to a small side entrance. Here they turned into a narrow, gloomy corridor that shelved down into darkness. Humber grabbed Fenn's hand as he pulled him past more of the wooden stanchions that propped up the low, jagged ceiling. When they were out of earshot, Humber glanced around, quickly lowering his voice and jerking his head towards the end of the cave. He lifted the candle so Fenn could see better.

"You've got sharp eyes. Notice anything here?"

"What?" Fenn asked. He couldn't see a thing other than a chunk of limestone sticking out like the prow of a boat, casting deep shadow to one side.

"Terras never check down here cos of these," Humber whispered, giving one of the wooden stanchions a soft kick. A shower of stone dust powdered from the roof. "If they ever did they might find a surprise. Well?" he asked.

Fenn stared and listened. All he could hear were the bangs and clatters reverberating up from the main cavern as the other units started work, but at that moment he felt a cold draught needle down the passage. The candle flame fluttered and ducked.

"You think we've been twiddlin' our thumbs while we waited for you to save us?" Humber smiled. "There's a tunnel."

"Under the Wall?" Fenn asked.

"No, out to sea," Humber answered sarcastically. "Terras nibbed a clever old fella a coupler months back. Knew the marsh and lie of the land. I worked this patch with him an' he told me a secret…" He motioned to Fenn to get nearer and Fenn leant in to hear. "He said this mine's not all flint. Said there'd be a seam of chalk right here! Sure enough, we found it. Soft as butter, an' almost as easy to scoop out! He started pickin' at it but a coupler weeks ago there was a rockfall an' his leg got well gammed up. Can't lift a pick no more; works at the sick-house now. I took up where he left off."

"Can I see?" Fenn asked excitedly. He'd never imagined it would be possible to get to the other side of the Wall.

"Nothin' *to* see. We stuffed it up with chippings an' rip-rap. Just in case a Terra came snoopin'. But it only needs one kick to knock it down."

"Does anyone else know?"

"A few. Ones I trust. Before Magpie said who you were, I already knew you were a good 'un. The way you looked out for those other kids. The way they looked to you. But there aren't many like you. The Terras got a tidy little scam here: extra rations for people who give them information. Extra rations for spies. And wanna know what information they want? Not who's causin' trouble but who's doin' good; who's helped someone out, who shared their rations, who did a double shift so someone could be with their family for a bit. The Terras use the Trusties to set Seaborn against Seaborn."

Fenn shook his head despondently. After thinking Moray was wrong about the Hellhulk prisoners fighting, it turned out he was right.

"Don't get that upside down neither." Humber said. "An evil place like this might make people do evil things, but people who snitch aren't all bad – they're just starvin'. There aren't many who hold out. That's why I couldn't tell everyone."

Humber's eyes shone, lamp-like in the gloom. He gripped Fenn's arm tightly.

"The Trusties will soon work out this unit hasn't been

199

cuttin' as much stone as before, so we have to move quick. Now's the perfect time. Two weeks ago, a hundred Terras were on night shift, last week it was fifty ... and tonight? Just a handful. That stupid fool Chilstone – he's got 'em all out on the marsh, chasin' his ghosts, lookin' for you!" he smiled mischievously. "When they don't have enough guards, they lock down the *Brimstone*. No guards on it at all. That's after rations have been doled out. That's when we act. But first we have to spread the word about you. A few Seaborn stormin' the mine? They'll be cut back by the Terras fast as you say snap! But once they all know the Demari boy's alive and kicking, then every Seaborn will fight until their last breath to get out!"

Before Fenn could answer, a sharp whistle echoed down the passageway.

"Back to work," Humber whispered. "Can't afford to have Terras pokin' around down here."

16

It was pitch-dark as they tramped back across the bridge towards the *Brimstone* after the shift, and the wind swept glugs of freezing seawater up over the wooden boards, drenching their feet. Fenn's head was full of plans to escape, but Gulper and Fathom talked about nothing but food. All they'd had to eat and drink all day was half a cup of water each, and a mouldy slice of rice bread.

"Do we get full rations? We got a full load in the dram," Gulper asked hopefully, holding his coat tight against the sleeting wind.

Humber shook his head, gesturing to the single crate of food being loaded onto the *Brimstone* ahead of the workers. "Not today," he said with a sigh, as the drawbridge ground shut behind them.

No Terras followed them inside the *Brimstone* tonight,

instead escorting the workers only as far as the drawbridge. Once that closed, Fenn heard the huge bolts being dragged into their slots and realised Humber was right: the *Brimstone* was on Lockdown.

As news of the dismal rations got out, people from every deck of the ship swarmed into the main hall to make sure they got a share. Instantly, fights and arguments clanged in ugly shouts across the hall and people jostled to get close to the only crate. When the *Brimstone* was on Lockdown it was a free for all. Their wrangles were eventually interrupted by a loud hollering as Magpie and a stout woman came stomping down the ladders, banging their iron ladles on the railings as they came.

"We the cooks – everyone knows we do the dolin' out!" Magpie yelled, brandishing her ladle at anyone who looked like they might disagree. The two women grabbed either side of the crate and hitched it up between them. They began to lug it back up to the kitchens, budging people out of the way with their pointy elbows that seemed specially sharpened for the purpose.

But Magpie hadn't counted on Lazlo. He stepped out of the shadows, blocking her way, his greasy lackey lurking by his side; an equally mean-looking man with a scar running from the corner of his mouth to one ear, giving him a permanent lopsided smile.

"Let me help you with that," Lazlo said, looking down at her with an unpleasant grin. Suddenly her ladle was in his hand. "Guess this makes me cook now." He smirked. "So I'll be doing the doling out." Immediately the rest of his cronies formed a circle around the crate like a wake of vultures. Lazlo calmly began to jemmy the lid off with the ladle handle.

"How 'bout this time, you leave somethin' for the littl' 'uns?" Magpie asked, nervously standing her ground. Fenn instantly moved forwards, but Humber grabbed his sleeve, pulling him back, silently shaking his head. Lazlo was not to be crossed.

Without even bothering to turn around, Lazlo lashed out with his free fist and Magpie went sprawling to the floor, blood spurting from her mouth. Lazlo tossed the ladle at her and it clattered in the hushed silence.

Before anyone could stop him, Fenn lurched forwards to help Magpie. Gulper, Fathom and Humber were only a few paces behind when Fenn reached her, helping her to her feet. Magpie quickly scrunched a fist of cloth against her bleeding lips. She was trembling with shock, but forced a smile.

"Din't hurt none!" she said stubbornly, her eyes glittering with pain.

"She's just a cook," Lazlo smirked, as he passed a huge

chunk of rice bread to one of his cronies. "Needs to learn to keep her mouth shut."

Pure and absolute hatred drenched Fenn. He felt anger flash electrically in his temples, as if his brain was actually overheating. Without thinking, he grabbed the ladle and swung it hard, striking Lazlo clean on the side of the head with one precise blow. Lazlo, the smile still playing on his lips, toppled unconscious to the floor. His cronies backed away, eyeing Fenn uncertainly. Everyone in the hall was silent until a lone man spoke up.

"Idiot!" he yelled. "Now we'll get rations docked completely. We can't take more punishments!" He sounded like he was about to cry.

"The Terras will punish us, whatever we do!" Fenn shouted furiously, glaring at the man who'd spoken out.

He searched the sea of faces for his friends, but the angry heat inside his head had made it hard to focus. An old woman, hobbling on a stick, pushed through the crowd to the front. She'd been one of those huddled and grumbling by the fire the first night Fenn arrived. She pointed a bony finger accusingly at him.

"You only arrived two days ago and you're already making trouble," she scowled, scooping the remains of her ragged shawl around her bony shoulders.

Just at that moment Amber clambered down a ladder

holding Tikki in her arms, coming to find out what the commotion was about. The old woman cast an eye over her, then turned back to Fenn. "If you're so worried about us starving, your pet otter would feed a few," she said, cackling.

Lazlo began to groan on the floor and his men stooped down to help him to his feet. Fenn looked around at the angry faces gaping at him and stepped up onto the crate.

"Get down, Fenn," Magpie hissed, tugging at his sleeve, but he ignored her.

"We should be trying to help each other, not fight each other!" he shouted over the crowd.

"Now he's telling us what to do!" the old woman said bitterly. "Who d'you think you are anyway?"

Trust your instinct, Halflin always said.

"I'm Fenn Demari," he said. "My parents were Tomas and Maya Demari." He pulled the key out from where it was hidden under his shirt, stretching the chain out so everyone could see. It flickered luminously in the dreary gloom, somehow seeming to glitter brighter than it ever had before.

A stunned silence engulfed the crowd, followed by a confusion of chatter and questions as people jostled forwards to get a better look at the pale, skinny boy standing before them, holding the famous Demari key.

"And so what if you are? The Resistance is dead!" growled one of Lazlo's men, full of bravado. He realised there'd be a vacancy if Lazlo died, and he planned to fill it.

Fenn took a deep breath. "The Resistance isn't dead! Because *we're* the Resistance! I am, you are," he pointed to the man who'd spoken out in the beginning. "She is," he pointed to Amber, helping Magpie stop the bleeding. "I'd been looking for the Resistance for months, before I realised it isn't someone else: it's in us already!" He banged his hand on his chest. "The Terra Firma want to destroy us, and they're getting us to do it for them. When the Wall's finally built, what do you think Chilstone's going to do with us all?"

There were murmurs of agreement from the crowd as Fenn's words sank in.

"The Terras say who lives, who dies, who eats, who starves, who gets to live behind the Wall! But our lives aren't something to be rationed out!"

There were a few cheers from the Sargassons and Fenn's friends.

"So if you want to live," Fenn continued, "listen to me! We must take back the Hellhulks and free everyone. Seaborns built the Walls; they have a right to be safe behind them!"

A cheer suddenly rippled through the whole crowd.

"The Sargassons are fighting the Terras on the marsh right now and the rest of us must stand with them! It doesn't matter if you're Sargasson, Venetian, Scotian … we are all Seaborn! Now is the time to unite; now is the time to fight back!"

Cheers reverberated around the hall, echoing off the iron bulkheads. But the old woman continued to glower at Fenn, rapping her stick repeatedly on a metal pipe, until the cheers eventually died out.

"Big words from a little boy," she wheezed. "But how exactly are we going to get over that giant Wall?"

Before Fenn could answer, Humber spoke up. "We're not goin' over. We're goin' *under*. My crew have dug a tunnel from the mine. Took us two months' sweat, but now we're through."

As word of this swept around the hall the crowd pressed in excitedly, eager to learn more. Fenn tucked the necklace back and jumped down from the crate, pushing through the crowds towards the drawbridge.

"All that's between us and freedom is this," he shouted, banging his fist on the door. "So let's break it down!"

A brawny Scotian, with muscles on his shoulders like he had a sack of boulders under his skin, lumbered over to a thick oak bench and wrenched it from its footings. He lifted it as though it were a twig and hoisted it onto his shoulder and the crowds parted to let him through, patting his muscles as he passed. A band of Sargassons gathered alongside him, like a roost of crows, to help hold it in position ready to use as a battering ram against the drawbridge. Groups of men were pulling other benches off their housings and dragging them to the door too.

Until now the Terras had always made them work in teams according to their race: Sargassons and Scotians, Caspians and Venetians. The Terras encouraged their apparent differences, pitting one group against another; always the broken against the downtrodden while the powerful reigned the same. But now they worked as one, together. Years of dragging the carts back from the mines had given them wiry muscles. The Scotian braced himself at the front and nodded, purple veins popping across his neck as he heaved his mountainous shoulder against the bench. Fenn and Fathom ran to join him and the battering crew. On the Scotian's count, they swung the benches back and punched them against the drawbridge. The huge metal slab that made the drawbridge shuddered and groaned; rivets bounced out and fell clanging onto the iron floor. Rust showered through the air, turning it a murky red. The oil in the hall lamps was running out and they flickered down to tiny matchhead flames, warping the men's shadows on the iron bulkheads so that they looked like giants.

"Again!" the crowd roared.

The men threw their anger once more behind the oak

benches; again they were showered with the fine red dust. Time and time again, they smashed the benches against the door until there was a sudden grinding split as one of the bolts outside bent and twisted away from the frame.

"Now this side!" Fenn shouted.

Immediately the teams of men hefted the benches over to the side where the second bolt still held true. Again they swung the benches together as one. At last the bolt twisted free, but somehow the vast iron door still stood strong.

"The centre!" Fenn ordered.

The men, rust-stained sweat tinting their shirts like blood, now swung the benches straight into the heart of the door. It only needed one true thrust for the drawbridge to finally burst open. It crashed down onto the bridge and a huge cheer rose up from the Seaborns. As the bridge was thrust down in the water two arcs of foaming water, like angels' wings, sprayed out from either side. But as the wings splashed down, the cheers died in the throats of the prisoners.

Facing them on the other side of the drawbridge, a unit of Terras was already waiting. They were wearing the full defensive gear that Fenn remembered from the Sweep on the Shanties; masks obscured their faces to protect them from disease and gauntlets covered their hands. The dog handlers were at the front, pulling back with all their strength on six savage Malmuts, which already strained to get at the prisoners. At the head of the unit stood the young captain from the Swampscrew. He hadn't counted on facing a full-scale riot without enough men to deal with it, but he held his nerve and ordered the Malmuts to be released.

The Malmuts hurled themselves over the jagged edges of the ripped drawbridge, snarling and growling, skidding on the sea-lashed floor. They were followed by the Terras, who drew their truncheons mid-leap, striking any prisoners as they landed. They didn't care who they hit; young children and old people ran away and tried to hide.

It was pandemonium. There was little light in the great hall, other than a faint shaft of dull moonlight where the drawbridge had been breached. As the Terras charged, brandishing truncheons, the Malmuts snapped their jaws blindly, confused and excited; they could smell fear everywhere.

Terrified mothers, clasping their crying children, scattered in fear, finding shelter in stairwells, trying to bundle their families to safety. Anyone fit enough tried climbing up the network of pipes above the bulkheads. But others, inspired by Fenn's speech and bravery, grabbed anything they could use as a weapon. They tore the treads from the ladders to throw, and the teams that had rammed the door used the same benches to push oncoming Terras back over the drawbridge, where they fell screaming into the water. A mob of sixty strong men charged out onto the pontoon bridge and took the fight to the remaining Terras.

As Terras and Seaborns battled, Fenn found himself being pushed further away from the drawbridge, back into the *Brimstone*. A few yards from him, the huge Scotian tore a chunk of piping away from the Hellhulk's side, and swung it like a cudgel, knocking one of the Malmuts off balance so that it skidded across the drawbridge, ramming three Terras off the side. Sargassons wrenched railings off walkways and used them like swords against any Terras trying to get beyond the first deck.

Fenn grabbed a stump of wood and swung it towards the head of a Malmut about to pounce at Amber, who was now backed against one of the ship's steel ribs, holding Comfort tight behind her and trying to keep a hold of Tikki, who was scrabbling from under her arm to get back to the safety of Fenn. But just as Fenn raised it to strike, the Malmut, confused by the ever-increasing smell of fear, sunk its teeth into the thigh of a Terra running past. The animals only knew who their masters were by the pain they inflicted, but when free, they bit and clawed at will. Tikki at last managed to break free of Amber's grip and scurried up to the pipes in order to see where Fenn was.

Realising he'd made a terrible mistake by letting the Malmuts off their leashes, the captain yelled to the handlers to recall them. Fenn quickly tried to push through the crowd to Amber and Comfort, but the Scotian suddenly collided with him in the gloom, stumbling away from two pursuing Terras. One of them lunged at the Scotian, but he was knocked off balance by another Malmut charging by, frothing at the mouth. The Terra's truncheon glanced off the Scotian's shoulder, but caught Fenn on his damaged eye. He crashed to the floor – Mattie's stitches were undone and the wound popped open again.

As Fenn gasped in pain, the Malmut skidded to a halt and turned back in the direction of his scent. This one seemed more alert; it stood, rooted to the spot, haunches quivering with excitement. It recognised more than fear this time – it remembered Fenn's scent from the hunt on the marsh. The air soured as the animal panted, its pupils roaming blanky in its opaque eyeballs. As it turned to leap, Fathom threw himself between Fenn and the brute. At the same moment, the Scotian swung the pipe against the Malmut's huge head. The Malmut fell on the floor yelping and the two Terras turned and fled, pursued by the Scotian, roaring bloodthirstily.

"Fenn!" Fathom cried, as he leant over, shielding Fenn. Hearing the name through the crowd, the Terra captain turned to face them.

"I'm OK!" Fenn struggled to stand.

"That's him!" the captain shouted, hurtling towards

them, but the Scotian had returned and barred his way.

At the same moment, hearing Fenn's voice in the darkness, Tikki bounded off the pipes and onto the captain's head, using it as a springboard for his next leap to where Fathom was pushing Fenn to the safety of the ship's wall. "They mustn't get you," Fathom hissed in his ear as he tore the precious necklace off Fenn's neck. Before Fenn could react, Humber and Magpie had grabbed him and yanked him away towards a side door.

Fenn struggled to get free, but Humber's grip was like an iron manacle around his arms. As they heaved him through the door to the lower decks, Fenn caught a last glimpse of the captain bearing down on Fathom before he was dragged into a pitch-black passageway. He was vaguely aware of a scurrying and squeaking behind them, and guessed Tikki must be following. The noise of the fighting dimmed as Fenn was hurried down stairwells he hadn't even known existed, deeper and deeper into the bowels of the ship. Rats scuttled ahead of their frantic steps like they were guiding their escape, until eventually they reached a passage lit by a single candle, ending with an iron door. They thrust it open and bundled Fenn inside.

"Hide him!" Humber shouted into the darkness. "Terras are coming!"

Then the door was slammed shut in Fenn's face.

17

Fenn turned immediately to try and get back out, but the door had been bolted shut from the outside. He felt something scratch his leg and looked down. It was Tikki, pawing at him to be picked up. Fenn leant down, speckling the floor with blood from his eye. He pressed the cuff of his sleeve against the wound, his head swimming, and gently put Tikki around his neck, letting him nuzzle against him and rubbing his cheek into his warm side. Tikki's fur always felt so soft; Fenn was flooded with gratitude that he hadn't been hurt.

Beyond him hung a piece of sacking. He pulled it back and found himself in a fire-lit, windowless room. Fenn knew he was in the ship's brig – the jail that had once been for Seaborns before the entire ship was made a prison. The air tasted of wet iron and along the sides were narrow, open cells each containing a simple wooden bed. A pot-bellied stove crackled at the end and condensation dripped from huge iron joists that criss-crossed the ceiling. Next to the stove was a bench glinting with bottles, and hanging over it was a battery of implements like carpenter's tools: saws, knives and clamps. Fenn realised the brig was now a sick-house for the ill or dying.

A gloomy passageway ran down one side of the stove and Fenn hurried towards it as fast as his dizziness would allow; his wounded eye was fattening from the Terra's blow and felt searingly hot. As he approached, he heard heavy, limping steps coming towards him, accompanied by the sound of a stick thumping on the ground. He remembered Humber saying he had a friend working here – the man who'd been hurt in a rockfall.

"Hello?" Fenn called. "I need to get out of here!"

The limping steps hesitated.

"Who's tha'?" replied a muffled voice, shaky and frightened. Fenn couldn't believe his ears.

Out of the shadows limped a ghost. Fenn's breath stuck in his chest and he couldn't breathe.

The ghost hobbled nearer, leaning perilously on a stick, the other hand outstretched. His lame leg dragged behind him, scuffing through the sawdust. Fenn backed away, choking on a sob. He had to be hallucinating. He dug his nails into his palm to break the spell. Hearing the voice in his head had been hard enough; he couldn't stand to dream that he was seeing him too.

"Is that mi' boy?" Halflin whispered.

He was as thin as a scratch – so much thinner. Older – so much older. But alive! He'd never looked so alive. Fenn took a huge gasp of air, suddenly propelled out of the dark grief he'd been drowning in ever since he heard his grandad was dead. Then he let out a howl, almost like the one he had as a baby when Halflin first saved him from the water. Halflin had reached him now and grabbed him, pulling him against his own thumping heart, cradling his head against his shoulder. As Fenn flooded with tears, he sagged against Halflin, trying so hard to speak but each time being ambushed by wracking sobs. Finally he stuttered out, "Lundy... said..." But he couldn't finish his sentence. Halflin slowly helped Fenn into a chair by the fire, where he slumped down. "She ... she said you'd died!"

"She thought tha' were truth," Halflin explained. "Poor thing. I 'eard she passed."

Tikki had been watching the old man with interest and sniffed at his ankles, squeaked at him, then jumped up and settled in Fenn's lap. "Yer caught yerself a mongoose," Halflin murmured as he began to wash the blood from Fenn's eye. Crying had made Fenn's breath gather in his chest like pleats of air, and he couldn't get the words out.

"Take a minute," Halflin told him and Fenn gently stroked Tikki's fur, making him purr. That sound had always warmed Fenn's heart.

"I ... I ... found him on the *Panimengro*," Fenn managed, his breath slipping out in a shuddering sigh. "I can't believe you're alive!"

"An' I can't believe yer here! Word was yer were on the Shanties, an' I believed it 'til the Punchlock got lit. Guessed it were you! Then rumour were yer'd got ter the Sargassons." Halflin grabbed a rag from the table and pressed it hard against Fenn's eye.

"I did! Moray helped me and my friends, but the Terras attacked, and we got away but—"

"Yer got caught." Halflin nodded. "Every Seaborn ends up here."

"Humber showed me the tunnel you started. Everyone's trying to break out, but the Terras are doing a Sweep."

"Lookin' fer yer?" Halflin said, alarmed.

Fenn nodded. "Humber and Magpie hid me down here..."

"Don't know no Magpie, but that Humber, he's a good 'un!" Halflin murmured.

"I've got to get back, my friends are still—"

"Yer not goin' nowhere," Halflin muttered as he pressed

the edges of the torn skin together firmly. "If the Terras know yer on the ship, we don't have long. They'll be down here soon." Halflin quickly began to wind the bandage around Fenn's head.

"Why did Lundy think you'd died?" Fenn asked while Halflin worked.

"She saw 'em get me on the patrol bound ter the *Warspite*, but I jumped overboard an' took me chance in the water. They thought I'd drowned. Got ter shore, laid low, then tried ter get a boat ter come an' fetch yer. Got caugh' an' landed 'ere."

He tied a knot in the bandage and checked his work, tilting Fenn's face against the light.

"Wha' time is it?" he suddenly asked. "Reckon it's dawn?"

"Not yet," Fenn answered.

Halflin nodded and put his fingers on his temples to help himself think.

"Tha' hurt still?" he asked, studying Fenn's face.

"A bit," Fenn said. It felt like his head was on fire.

"Well, I got summat ter take the edge off tha'."

Halflin quickly fumbled along the bench until his fingers found a small glass bottle hidden behind the others, containing what looked like purple syrup. He uncorked it and gave it to Fenn to drink.

"Knock it back quick, it's bitter as cud."

He watched Fenn grimace as he swallowed the lot, then he helped him stand up. Tikki fell off Fenn's lap with an angry chatter, but Halflin just nudged him out of the way with the toe of his boot. Quick as the two of them could manage, he guided Fenn down the dark passage by the side of the fire. In the shadows behind them, Tikki scampered at a safe distance from Halflin's boot; he seemed to know instinctively that he must keep quiet around the stumbling old man.

"Is this another way back up?" Fenn asked, feeling his way through the gloom.

"Yep," Halflin mumbled as he stepped through a door-way into a second narrow corridor. He bolted the door hard behind him and they were plunged into complete blackness. Fenn felt like he couldn't breathe; he started to feel sick.

"Grandad…?"

"Yep?" Halflin answered, stubbornly limping ahead.

"I feel strange."

"Well, yer took a knock, din't yer?" Halflin mumbled as he tapped down the corridor. Fenn heard a bolt being passed back and another door creaked open, revealing a gloomy room with a long wooden trolley, on which three large rice sacks were already lined up. Around the ceiling were the remains of bars where more cells had once been. The far end of the room was made up of a large goods lift with a square door and a heavy crank handle on the right.

"Sit there," Halflin told him, lifting him under the arms onto the edge of the trolley. Fenn watched woozily as Halflin began to shunt the sacks along to make space. His eyelids suddenly drooped and he was overcome with a desire to lie down. He forced himself to stay upright.

"But…" he just managed to say through his grogginess. "I have to get back to…"

"I have ter get you out," Halflin said firmly, drawing his hand over his face, as if trying to wipe away the Punchlock and all the woes it had brought him. He grunted as he heaved the next two sacks further down the trolley. "So I give yer a little sleepwort," he said quietly. "Din't like ter trick yer, but I know yer too well. Yer'd never leave yer friends, an' tha'll get yer killed."

Fenn struggled to stand up, but his joints felt like they were loosening, like a puppet having its strings snipped. Halflin only needed to give him the gentlest nudge for Fenn to slide sideways down onto the cool stone. He fought to keep awake, rolling his head onto his cut so pain would make him sharp again. When that didn't work, he tried to bite his tongue but his teeth kept missing their mark.

"Don't fight it," Halflin instructed. "Sleepwort slows the heart. Makes yer feel dead – makes yer look dead." He lifted

Fenn's feet up onto the trolley. "Viktor'll be here soon ter get the next load up on deck, then off ter the bone-barge. There'll be a coupler Malmuts sniffin' round fer sure, but they'll smell nothin'. Yer'll be dead ter them."

Fenn could only blink as he watched Halflin. Now he realised what was in the sacks.

"Don't be 'fraid. They can't hurt yer," he said. "When yer wake up, Viktor'll take yer somewhere safe 'til dust settles. He still owes me. I got his wife an' kid ter safety once. After this we're quits. Don't be mad at him for dumpin' yer on the Shanties. He'd only do that if 'e 'ad ter."

Halflin shook out a large empty sack, and began to pull it up around Fenn's feet like a sleeping bag. Seeing that he was soon to be covered made Fenn all the more desperate. He mustered every last fibre in his body to lift his head and look at Halflin.

"Come with me..." he just managed to say, before his tongue flopped uselessly in his mouth. Halflin shook his head.

"Sleepwort would slaugh'er a worn heart like mine. Peaceful death, but I ain't ready yet. Besides, an old man wiv a gammy leg will geddus both killed." Halflin reached out and touched Fenn's hair with the tips of his fingers. His hands were trembling.

Now or never, he told himself. *Now or never.* He squatted down on his heels so his face was level with Fenn's.

"Got summat ter say. Blink if yer can hear."

Fenn blinked.

"Lundy always wanted me ter tell yer this – an' she were right."

Halflin swallowed. He'd never tried to win Fenn's love, but he didn't want his hate either. He hoped Fenn would forgive him. His voice was raw.

"Yer folks weren't me kin. I'm not yer grandad. I'm nuffin' ter do with the Demaris, 'cept that I sunk their barge; damn me for ever … an' then I found yer!"

Halflin let out a rasping laugh of amazement, remembering the fateful day their paths had crossed.

"Like dead in the water yer were, but yer took a breath an' yer lived again! We've both of us 'ad all our second chances, boy. Yer lived – an' I got ter tell yer the truth. Should've told yer years ago mind, but kept losin' me nerve."

Fenn struggled to stay awake but his body felt like it was being clawed downwards, somewhere deep and quiet; into the quagmires of sleepwort sleep, shadowy, cool as a coffin. He could barely even open his eyes now.

Halflin stood up and unwound his scarf.

"I know I did wrong ter try an' keep yer, when yer weren't mine ter keep," he said, tucking the scarf under Fenn's cheek for a pillow. "Strange; all 'em years we 'ad

222

in our little hut, with no one but each other fer company, yet I never foun' one momen' ter tell yer."

He bit his lip at his weakness.

"An' I knowed tha' would've bin safest. If yer knowed the truth, then maybe yer never would've come back."

Sleepwort had thickened Fenn's thoughts into slurry, but he could hear every last word Halflin said. Before he finally lost consciousness he thought, *I would always have come back...*

Then everything melted together into a sludge of red and black, marsh and river, whales and Wall, Tikki and friends, water and stone. A tear rolled out of Fenn's eye onto Halflin's hand, but the skin there was too calloused for Halflin to feel something so small. Instead he stroked Fenn's hair once more before taking his hand away as if he had no right to even touch Fenn. He allowed himself to look at Fenn for just a few seconds more, then got on with what needed to be done.

He went to the shaft, opened the door and yanked a rope-pull. Somewhere high up a bell clanged, echoing down the shaft: Halflin's signal to Viktor that he was ready. The lift could only be operated from the outside by two crank handles: one in the basement and one up on deck.

A few seconds later came the sound of grinding cogs and wheels as Viktor lowered the crate. While Halflin had been talking to Fenn, Tikki hid silently in the shadows, but as soon as the old man's back was turned, he jumped up on the trolley and wriggled down in the sack, squirming beneath Fenn's jacket and lying very still – he wasn't letting Fenn out of his sight. The rumbling in the shaft grew louder; there wasn't much time. Halflin took out a black glass bottle and tucked it in Fenn's coat pocket, then pulled the rest of the sack up over Fenn's head and tied it with a slip knot that could be quickly undone.

A clanking sound echoed in the room and a crate appeared in the shaft opening. Halflin quickly wheeled the trolley over and heaved the first sack inside, trying not to bump it on the wooden sides. It took another five minutes before he'd got the other inside, by which time sweat had beaded on his brow. When it was Fenn's turn, he rested his hand on the hessian one last time before pulling on the bell rope again to signal Viktor to crank the crate back up.

As he watched the crate disappear up into the darkness, he suddenly remembered the little mongoose that had followed Fenn in. He shut the door to the shaft and stumbled back down the corridor, whistling into the shadows, trying to remember if it had a name. He'd have to find it; the little thing had looked so scared. It would need looking after.

18

Something stung acridly in Fenn's nose and throat, and he spluttered up from the depths of unconsciousness. He felt like he'd been underwater for a long time, as if his body had been shipwrecked, leaving his mind floating away like a piece of jetsam in a vast, blank sea. Vague memories slopped over him as he was lifted on a swell of queasiness with each breath. All he could see was the purple-spotted orange light through the shield of his own eyelids. As his mind came back into focus, he wondered if he was still on the *Brimstone* and if Halflin was still there. He had so much he wanted to ask him; so much he didn't understand. But of all his questions only one mattered; who did either of them belong to if not each other? He was angry too, not at Halflin's trickery but at his own stupidity in not expecting it. He should have known Halflin would always be one step ahead.

Fenn managed to open one eyelid and saw something glinting close by, then he felt something move by his hand and was overjoyed to realise Tikki was there too, sniffing and licking his palm, trying to rouse him. Gradually the vague shape in front of him sharpened into a face. Fenn wouldn't have recognised him if it weren't for the F-shaped scar, sticking out even more brutally now that his head was shaved so close the skin had been nicked in many places. Veins snaked beneath the stubble like the grey ghosts of braids he once had knotted there. It was Viktor.

Fenn was lying on a bench in the cabin of a tug, even smaller than the one Halflin had used to tow Sunkmarked boats back to the Punchlock. To one side, steam shot from the spout of a green kettle dancing on the stove's hotplate, and next to the bench a small wooden table showed signs of a recent meal – a crust of rice bread and a few too-hard beans scattered over an enamel plate. At the front of the cabin stood the ship's wheel; charts and maps showing the coastline of East Isle were nailed to every beam, each of them bearing the Terra Firma stamp.

"It's hartshorn," Viktor said as he re-stoppered the bottle he'd been waving under Fenn's nose before stowing it away in the table drawer. "You'd call them smelling salts – a gift from Halflin. Sharp now?" he asked, digging his hard hands under Fenn's arms and hoisting him up to a sitting position. "So, the *Panimengro*'s tosher was Fenn Demari all along!" Viktor smiled, clapping his shoulder.

"I have to go back," Fenn said immediately, trying to stand, but his sleep-slack muscles weren't ready for that yet and he instantly toppled over. Viktor helped pick him up and propped his jacket under one side to keep him from rolling over. Then he stomped over to the stove where he clattered the kettle against a tin mug.

The long sou'wester Fenn had never seen him take off had gone, and in its place Viktor was dressed in the slug-grey boiler suit that all Fearzero workers were forced to wear. The one he wore – and the spare Fenn had spotted hanging on the nail by the door – were the only clothes he had; the Terra Firma owned him now. On his back was emblazoned a large Terra Firma insignia: a sharp-edged red triangle with a black T and F in the centre. Coming back to Fenn with the steaming drink, he caught Fenn's eye and shrugged as if it didn't bother him so much.

"What of it? So the old devil rides my back," he muttered. "At least I'm alive." He pushed the mug across the table.

"I need to help my friends, and Halflin too," Fenn said.

Viktor jerked his chin towards the mug. "Drink before talk. You look green-gilled. Don't want spew on my table," he grumbled, shoving the mug at him and slopping the contents. "Careful, it's meski," he warned, clenching his fist.

Fenn still looked blank. "Living with Sargassons and still not learnt our tongue? Meski means 'strong'. Very strong!"

Fenn nodded and knocked it back in one scalding gulp. It was like swallowing nettle and wasp stings mixed together: sweet, sharp, hot and minty, like the syrup Halflin used to spoon on the back of Fenn's tongue when he had a sore throat. The drink seemed to blaze into all the fuggy nooks and crannies of his mind, making his thinking clear and sharp.

"You listen to me!" Fenn demanded. "You have to take me back now!"

Viktor returned to the wheel and peered through the soot-smeared windows. Outside the sun was beginning to set and the sky was mottling to a deep blue.

"I promised I'd get you as far away as possible. Halflin wants you safe. We all do."

"To West Isle?"

"In the *Crescent*?" Viktor laughed, slapping the wheel scornfully. "She's not the *Panimengro*! She can only just manage the sea between the Hellhulks and the *Warspite* – that's all this beach-hugger's good for. Halflin said to get you on another Gleaner. The *Sastimos* is waiting for you."

Viktor locked the wheel before opening the door and stepping onto the narrow deck. Fenn staggered out after him.

228

"Why don't yer make yerself useful? Skeg for her lights; she's docked here somewhere," Viktor mumbled, passing him a telescope to look through. Meanwhile he checked the ropes running through the tyre fenders that bounced around the edge of the little boat.

Fenn lifted the brass to his eye: they were only a mile off the shore. He quickly swung back towards the *Brimstone* and the *Hercules*; smoke plumed like storm clouds from the *Brimstone*'s stern. Further out to sea, he could just make out distant twinkling lights on the old familiar shape of the *Warspite*. Then he turned the telescope to scan the many bays and inlets fretting the coastline. Almost immediately he recognised the very tributary he and his friends had come into when they sailed the *Salamander* back. In the fading light, he spied a darker outline of a boat, tucked away in the reeds.

"She's there," he said, pointing.

"Your yews were always sharp," Viktor said approvingly. "Need to make this quick. Gotta be back by dawn. We're towing the *Warspite* to the *Brim* at first light. Then it's me that has to get rid of the body."

"What?" Fenn asked, frowning.

"Chilstone won't want no one to see it." He sucked his teeth thoughtfully as he steered the tug into the neck of the creek.

"What body?"

"The kid they took off the *Brim* – the one pretending to be you!" Viktor shook his head at Fenn like he was stupid. Fenn stared at him dumbfounded. Viktor shrugged. "He's either very brave ... or very stupid."

Fenn touched his bare neck and the necklace's absence. He felt sick as he remembered Fathom's words. *They mustn't get you!*

"...either way, it's good for us that Chilstone thinks he's got you," Viktor thought aloud, as he peered ahead into the gloom. "Shouldn't be any patrols out on the rivers tonight. Not with the execution, an' the rest of the Terras tryin' to settle the riots on the *Brim*."

"Execution? Chilstone won't kill him? He'll know he's got the wrong boy! He's seen me. He knows about my eyes." Fenn's face was white as milk.

"Chilstone will know, but so what?" Viktor mused. His eyes were lifeless and jaded. Fenn realised in an instant he'd given up all hope of fighting. "The boy is supposed to look like you. So long as Chilstone's got the key, got a boy everyone thinks is you? It's enough to crush the Resistance for ever."

At that moment, Viktor's attention was caught by a sycamore seed, spinning down onto the deck and he picked it up, idly shredding its flimsy wings as he spoke.

"Up there on the *Warspite*'s scaffold? Think that lot down on the *Brim* will know if it's you – the last Demari – or some other kid? Most of 'em are half-blind from the scurvy anyway. Chilstone knows that. No, the old devil will put on a show – get some lights sparkling on the gibbet. The riots will be over before they started if the Seaborns got no one to fight for." He sighed deeply and flicked what was left of the seed over the rail, scrutinising Fenn to see if he understood.

Fenn felt like time had suddenly slowed right down and he leant on the side of the cabin, feeling sure he was going to throw up for real this time. Viktor cocked him a warning eyebrow. "Down there," he snapped, jerking his head towards the stern. "Don't you puke on my deck."

Fenn stumbled to the back of the tug and gripped the spindly rail, letting the cold steel pinch his mind into focus. He wasn't going to waste time being sick. He considered jumping overboard and swimming to the *Warspite*, but she was just a speck out at sea, and if the tide was against him, he'd never make it in time. He had to make Viktor take him and he ran back inside.

"*Please*, Viktor. I'm begging you. You have to help me."

Viktor ignored him, letting the wheel glide lazily through his hands. "Please," Fenn begged. "The boy Chilstone's got? He's my friend. I have to save him!"

Viktor pretended he couldn't hear, staring ahead at a

flock of wild ducks that were startled by the tug, swooping up from the reeds to fly inland. Seeing he wasn't listening, Fenn grabbed Viktor's arm but Viktor brushed him off, his face hard as a hatchet. Fenn grabbed him again and this time Viktor whipped around. His eyes glinted with contempt.

"I've given everything to you and your family!" he spat, shoving Fenn in the chest with the flats of his hands.

"Halflin saved *your* wife and child!" Fenn shouted back.

Viktor took a single step and grabbed Fenn by the scruff of his jacket, yanking him up so they were nose to nose. Gripping Fenn's collar with one white-knuckled fist, he pointed at the scar down his cheek. Fenn winced to see it up close; the flesh seemed to bubble, and looked painful and raw.

"You never stop to wonder why Chilstone came after my wife and little 'uns in the first place? Or how I got my very own Demari key?" he asked bitterly, his breath hot on Fenn's face. "Not so pretty as the golden trinket you managed to lose, eh?" Viktor dropped Fenn back down, and stood trembling in his fury. He rubbed his hands over the scabbed stubble of his scalp. "I paid an ugly price."

In that second, Fenn understood. Ever since he'd met Viktor, he had thought the F had been made by a TF branding iron being pressed into the flesh. But now he saw it properly, it wasn't an F but the crude shape of a key; only the shank and the two pins. Chilstone had used the Demari

232

symbol of hope to brand all members of the Resistance, as Viktor had once been. That way he'd always know who his enemies were.

"It was only these that kept me alive," Viktor said, thumping his strong hands on the ship's wheel. "As long as the Terra Firma need captains who understand this stretch of pani, I'm safer than the rest. I got to keep my life. I can't ask for more."

With that, he hunched back over the wheel and returned his gaze to the river. The *Sastimos* was only a few hundred yards away now.

"I'm sorry," Fenn said. "Halflin didn't say."

"He was too busy staying alive. That's how he survived; clanked down with you, keeping schtum." Viktor shrugged, not even bothering to look at Fenn. "Anyway, all that's done now. You take the wheel. Cut the engine and punt us in. I need to signal; let them know it's us." His eyes were empty and dark. Fenn realised there would be no persuading Viktor; his mind was set.

Viktor took the lamp and left Fenn in the shadows. Fenn watched as he leant over the starboard rail, held the lamp high, then quickly covered the glass with a black cloth three times, letting the light shine brightly for just a few seconds – a signal to the crew on the *Sastimos* that a friend was approaching. With Fenn now at the wheel, they continued to chug up the river, slowly curving back into the marsh. Ahead, Fenn spotted the jetty he and his friends had seen just before they found Hill Farm, except it was nearly under water now.

When they were near enough, Fenn cut the engine and stepped out onto the deck. The sun had almost gone, and just the tip of it showed, as if it were drowning in the sea. Fenn hitched down one of the heavy wooden poles and pushed it down into the water, gently punting the tug between the darkening reeds. As he did so, he glanced upriver, frowning as a heron swooped towards them. At the last minute it swerved and followed the V-shaped flight of ducks they'd seen earlier, flying inland. It was an ill-omen for a heron to pass over a boat, so Viktor grinned at their good fortune, then signalled to the *Sastimos* once more, holding the lamp even higher and craning his neck as he scanned for a response from the other boat.

Finally, Fenn noticed a tiny flicker glimmering like a glow-worm in the reeds as the *Sastimos* signalled back to them, and at that exact moment, Viktor felt the full force of Fenn's hands whack into his back. Viktor was already leaning out far enough for it to need only one thrust upwards to tip him over the edge of the rail, lamp and all.

It was just a five-feet drop into the weedy water and Fenn was already running back along the narrow side deck when he heard the splash and Viktor's yell. He grabbed the never-used lifebuoy, now lichen green, and flung it in Viktor's direction, then raced back into the cabin. He twisted the key and started the engine again, and the little tug coughed back into life. By the time Viktor surfaced, spluttering threats at Fenn and trying to swim back, the tug was already ploughing back down the river.

"Come back!" Viktor hollered, but Fenn never even heard it over the tug's engines. All that mattered was saving Fathom. He whistled to Tikki, who scampered up onto his shoulders.

"Let's go," he said, steering the tug back towards the open sea and the *Warspite*.

19

Fenn was so attuned to the inky-blackness of the marsh that he could see nearly as well at night as in the daytime. As soon as he left the river, he draped sailcloth over anything that glinted – the way Magpie had done the first night aboard the *Panimengro*, when they hadn't wanted to be spotted. The *Crescent* was small and easy to steer, and he took it out to sea, before looping back to approach the *Warspite* from the port side, where he would be hidden from a sighting from the shore. At the *Warspite's* bow, Fenn discovered four more tugs already in position, waiting to tow the great ship to dock in the shallow channels at daybreak, but was relieved to see they were all dark, their crews asleep. He dropped the *Crescent's* anchor a few yards from the *Warspite's* massive anchor chain; so enormous, seagulls perched inside its iron links.

He slipped on the spare boiler suit, tucking the overlong trousers into his boots. His reflection in the black windows showed that only his hair stood out. He found Viktor's balaclava on a bent nail, yanked it over the Sargasson braids and rolled the edges up tightly. He ran outside and, spotting a grappling iron, grabbed it and swung it over towards the *Warspite*, where it hooked it in the anchor chain. Then he went back inside and lifted Tikki gently onto the table, pushing a few scraps of rice bread his way.

"You stay put. I've got to get over there." Fenn jerked his head through the cabin window where the *Warspite* loomed up out of the sea.

Tikki twitched his nose at him quizzically, sitting up on his hind legs and tapping his paw on Fenn's hand. Fenn gave him a kiss and checking he still had his knife, gently closed the door, ran across the deck and stepped up onto the rail. He was just about to swing his leg over when he heard scratching behind him. It was Tikki, standing on his hind legs on the rail.

"How did you get out?" Fenn scolded.

He scooped up Tikki – he didn't have time for games of hide-and-seek – and ran back to the cabin, scanning for ways Tikki had got out. It was a mystery; all the windows were closed, but then the grille in the cabin door caught his eye. The slats didn't look big enough for Tikki to squirm through, yet that must have been what he'd done. Fenn smiled at Tikki's smartness; he must have remembered he could squeeze through a grille from when Fenn pushed him to safety on the sinking drifter. He grabbed some rags and stuffed them into the slats. He kissed Tikki goodbye a second time and carefully closed the door.

He was already half way over the rail when another bout of furious chattering came from behind him. This time Tikki actually hissed at Fenn for his betrayal.

"How did you get out?" Fenn hissed back.

He only just managed to grab Tikki this time before he scampered off, and Fenn stomped back into the cabin and settled Tikki on the table. Thinking he'd won, and Fenn was going to stay now, Tikki began rubbing his head into Fenn's hand to get a stroke and a cuddle. Fenn cupped his hands around his furry head, trying to will Tikki to understand what had to be done.

"I've got to get Fathom, and I've got to do it on my own. It's too dangerous for you. Don't follow!" He finished with a harshness in his voice that Tikki had never heard before.

With that, he gave Tikki a last kiss, ran out and closed the door. He was about to run down the deck again when he had second thoughts. He needed to see how Tikki was getting out or they'd be here all night. He crept back to the cabin and peeped over the ledge.

Fenn watched as Tikki took a run up and hurled himself heroically at the door. He heard a thump, as if Tikki had fallen. Immediately Tikki was up on the table again, throwing himself at the cabin door a second time. This time Fenn heard a click as the handle went down, and the cabin door swung slowly open, revealing Tikki dangling from the handle. He had realised he could use his body weight to pull the handle down.

As the door swung forwards, Tikki saw that Fenn had been spying on him. He let out a ferocious shriek and dropped to the deck to escape, but Fenn caught him before he even landed.

Fenn put him back in the cabin, gave him another last kiss, and this time wedged a deck-broom under the door handle. Then he climbed over the *Crescent*'s rail a final time and shimmied across to the anchor chain. He'd been so distracted by Tikki, he hadn't had time to think about being scared. He started the hard climb up the anchor chain towards the hawsepipe, that glinted in the side of the bow halfway up the *Warspite*'s hull.

It was a good fifty feet higher from where he was and the further he climbed, the harder the wind blew. Although each link of the anchor chain was as thick as a tree trunk, they were slippery with seaweed. Halfway up, he paused for breath, hooking his leg through the chain and giving each arm a rest. He stuffed his frozen fingers into his mouth and puffed some life into them. Straightening his legs out hard against the hull, he looked along the side of the *Warspite* to check where the goods winch was. If he got Fathom out, the winch could provide an escape route.

A few feet above the hawsepipe he could see the steel boarding ladder. He steadied himself, then leapt, only just grasping the last freezing steel rung, rubbed satin-smooth by the countless Terras tramping up and down it over the years. He hung for a second before clawing up and peering over the deck rail. It was deserted; the only sound came from the Scragnet creaking. He tumbled over the rail, searching for some way to get below deck. In the shadows between the gun turrets, he spied a door and hurried towards it. He was halfway along the deck, keeping to the shadows, when it suddenly swung open and the first of a troop of Terras marched through, a lone figure in their midst. Fenn's heart skipped a beat. He knew who it was, catching the metal glinting in the moonlight: Chilstone.

By the side of the turrets, a deckhand had left their mop and pail, and Fenn grabbed them, as if he'd just finished swabbing down the deck himself. He walked on towards the door but as he passed Chilstone and his men, he couldn't help but sneak a glance at Chilstone's left hand.

It was gloved and there was nothing to see, but as Fenn walked on he sensed a movement from Chilstone, and knew it had been a mistake to look. His heart was thumping as he passed the Scragnet, only vaguely aware of the pull of the metal pail towards the vast magnet, and then he was at the door. He'd made it! The door banged shut behind him and he leant against it panting. Then he scrambled down the steel stairs, three steps at a time, praying the prison-brig in the *Warspite* was in the guts of the ship, the same as it was in the *Brimstone*. If the layout was identical and Fathom was down there, Fenn would have to think of how to get out. He remembered the shaft that Halflin had used to get him off the *Brimstone*. He hoped all Fearzeros had them: they could escape that way.

Inside the *Warspite*, it was a maze of corridors and passages, with nothing to mark one from the other and Fenn had no sense of where he was; he only knew he always needed to head down. After dropping through layer after layer of the *Warspite*'s decks, he finally reached the bottom and found a short passage, so narrow and pokey he could have touched each side just by bringing his elbows up. It stank; the air was murky grey with the fumes from diesel and the kerosene lamps that lit the windowless interiors. He remembered Halflin comparing Fearzeros to sharks, always swimming in order to stay alive. Even when at a standstill, the *Warspite*'s propellers still turned to keep the tonnage of iron from sinking.

Fenn ran to the end of the passage and turned left then right, before realising he was no nearer to finding the brig. He turned back and retraced his steps, trying to find the passageway he came in by, when suddenly a siren blared out of the speakers on every wall. A door opened and a Terra ran out, pulling on his boots, hammering on every door he passed.

"All hands on deck. We're off to the *Brimstone* boys!" Taking Fenn for just another lowly deckhand, he thumped him on the chest and gave a cheery thumbs up. It was like they were going on an outing.

From every direction Fenn heard doors clanking open as the Terras worked their way up the stairs at either end of the tight passageway. Fenn ducked into a gloomy side passage as the corridor swarmed with Terras jostling along, swearing at being called to deck in their downtime.

"So Chilstone's crack unit can't handle a few sparky Seaborns," one of them crowed as he ran by.

"We'll show 'em how it's done," his friend replied, laughing.

Once the corridor cleared, Fenn ran in the opposite direction, until he spotted the steel door of the prison-brig. He took a deep breath and stepped through; this was going to be the hard bit.

It was a low, small room, lined with cells either side, just like the *Brimstone*'s sick-house except in place of the pot-bellied stove, sat a pot-bellied Terra, filling in paperwork at a tiny desk. The pink tab of his tongue stuck out on his lip as he concentrated on writing in a ledger with the last stub of a pencil.

"They want the Demari boy up on deck," Fenn said.

"What, now?" the guard mumbled, without bothering to look up.

"You heard the siren. I'm late already!"

"That's what the siren was for?" he grumbled as he got up and ambled towards another door into a corridor. Fenn followed a pace behind. "Not s'posed to release prisoners without two guards," he muttered.

"Tell Chilstone – he's already been waiting five minutes," Fenn snapped, trying to sound as gruff and old as possible.

At Chilstone's name, the guard moved quickly, unlocking a door into a long room. In a cell at the far end, by a goods lift, Fenn could see Fathom, lying on the floor, face to the wall. The guard fumbled with the keys and twisted one in the cell lock. Hearing the key in the door, Fathom woke up. As he sat up and faced them, Fenn put his fingers to his lips.

"He'll have to be cuffed," the guard said. Fenn leant in close and softly unclipped the guard's key chain, keeping hold of the end.

"Out!" the guard grunted at Fathom, jerking his thumb over his shoulder.

As the cell door swung open, Fenn suddenly barrelled against the guard's bulky side with all the force he could muster, pitching him into the cell. The guard staggered forward and Fathom bunched into a low ball, so that the guard toppled over him, hitting his head on the wall and crashing to the floor, where he lay stunned. Fathom was out in a flash, slamming the door shut as Fenn turned the key in the lock. They hugged quickly but Fenn was already dragging Fathom towards the lift.

"How did you get here?" Fathom asked.

"No time now," Fenn said, as he began cranking the lift handle. A loud rumble sounded as the crate trundled down.

"What's the plan?" Fathom asked.

"Get in this lift to the top deck, then climb down the anchor chain. Got a tug waiting: the *Crescent*. Tikki's locked in the cabin," Fenn gasped.

"Thought I was meant to be saving *you*!" Fathom said. With a final turn of the handle, the crate appeared in the opening that was cut into the shaft.

"You go first!" Fenn said, but Fathom didn't move.

"Why can't we both go?"

"Cos we can't winch it up from inside. Once you've got to the top, I'll jerk the rope to let you know I'm ready and you winch me up," Fenn explained, pushing Fathom into the crate.

Before he could argue, Fenn started winching the crate back up. "If something goes wrong," he yelled up the shaft, "don't wait! You have to get back to the *Brimstone* to help the others! Tell them to keep fighting!"

It was hard work, but finally Fenn felt the pulley ropes tighten – the lift had reached the top deck. Fenn waited impatiently as Fathom began cranking the crate back down. At last it arrived and he clambered inside and took the rope. But before he could give Fathom the signal, a pair of gloved-fists had grabbed him.

"Gotcha!" the Terra smirked. "Let's get him up on deck boys. Double rations for us tonight!" He ran a wet tongue over his lips.

Two other Terras gripped Fenn's arms, and before he knew what was happening, he was being hauled up the steps, so rough and fast that the tops of his boots strummed the treads. The door to the top deck opened and a blast of wet, salty air slapped his face.

"Considering you're not even Sargasson, you're very slippery, Fenn Demari. I was starting to doubt we'd ever meet again." Chilstone had his back to Fenn as he looked out over the coastline.

Speak for yourself. I knew we would, the voice in Chilstone's head muttered.

The breeze had picked up a little, and the storm clouds were scudding across the face of the moon. The *Warspite*'s deck was rinsed with a cold blue light as Chilstone turned to face him.

"I thought it was you. No one else would have dared to look straight at me."

Actually, it was me who worked it out, muttered the voice resentfully. *Credit where credit's due.*

Chilstone nodded and raised his hand slightly, as if he needed quiet to think. He smiled at Fenn and glanced along to where a gibbet had been erected on the starboard side of the ship.

"I had a feeling you'd come back for your friend. Loyalty is an enduring fault of the Demaris, it seems." He snapped his fingers at the guards to bring Fenn closer. When they were still a pace away, he raised his hand for them to stop. Gently pressing his cane under Fenn's chin, he tried to push it up.

Fenn resolutely looked at the ground. Not because he was scared of meeting Chilstone's eye, but because he knew Chilstone wanted to have fun with him before he killed him. He remembered the feral cat he'd once seen behind the hut, relentlessly tormenting a shrew; dropping its paw down on the creature's tail, then releasing it just long enough for the shrew to think it had a chance of escape, before patting it back again. In fact Chilstone's cruel instinct might work in his favour; the longer he had his fun, the longer Fenn had to think about escape and the better chance Fathom had of getting well away.

Chilstone began tapping the cane upwards with the words, "Chin up, chin up, chin up!" A little harder each time, until Fenn had to face him. "You have your mother's eyes," he murmured.

And his father's defiance, the voice hissed. *He was never afraid of you either.*

Chilstone shook it away. He'd been looking forward to interrogating Fenn on his own. He couldn't listen to the voice now.

"Why do you hate me so much?" Fenn asked.

"I don't hate you especially. I hate all Seaborns," Chilstone replied silkily.

"Why?"

"They killed my daughter, crippled me... Isn't that enough?" Chilstone asked, with a look of genuine surprise.

"But that was the Resistance," Fenn replied. "And they were driven to it."

From somewhere beyond the *Warspite*'s bow, Fenn thought he caught the distant sound of a high-pitched whine. At the same moment, one of the Terras on lookout ran back down the deck, a look of panic spreading over his face.

"Sir?" he said. Chilstone put up his hand and the Terra fell silent.

"Seaborns … Resistance … they're the same thing. Isn't that what *you* preach? You've been busy carrying on their good work." Chilstone pulled off his left glove. Fenn flinched at what he'd done: two crude pegs of welded steel pipe and wire replaced the fingers he'd lopped off. "Know what I overheard one of my own men saying the other day? That there wouldn't be much left of me soon."

Then we killed him, the voice muttered. Chilstone smiled. At least you could say that for the voice; it understood him.

"I had no choice," Fenn cried. "You would've killed me."

"Sir, it's important!" the Terra tried again.

Tell them to stop interrupting! the voice hissed. Chilstone glared at the Terra, then turned back to Fenn.

"And what choice do I have? There are hundreds of Seaborns willing to kill me, so long as you're alive." He looked Fenn over quizzically, as if trying to find the answer to a difficult sum he'd been struggling with, frowning and tilting his head to one side.

"How did you even know I existed?" Fenn asked.

A strange flash passed over Chilstone's face, something between triumph and melancholy. "You have your mother to thank for that…" he began.

Don't tell him! the voice demanded. *Not yet!* But Chilstone wasn't in the mood for teasing.

"She told me where to find you. Pleaded with me to save you. But the barge had already been sunk."

Fenn's pictured his mother desperately trying to save him. How frightened she must have felt. But Chilstone was intent on remembering his own misery and didn't notice the expression on Fenn's face.

Dawn was approaching and the sky was turning from deepest sapphire to the darkest plum-pink. Chilstone sighed regretfully.

"With hindsight I should have left well alone. Sometimes I wonder if it would have been better if I had. Ironic, isn't it, that my looking for you made you more real to people? You could have mouldered away in that old hovel, and none of us would have been any the wiser. None of this would have happened."

He shifted position, easing his head first to the left then right, loosening the cricks in his neck.

"But I couldn't help myself. I thought the Sargassons might be hiding you and went searching, when all the time it was old Halflin. If you look at it one way, I *made* you." The strange expression flitted over his face again.

"And what about my parents?" Fenn asked, his voice shaking with anger as he thought again of his mother. She must have died thinking he was dead too.

"They refused to give me the names of those who killed my daughter, so I had to make an example of them. A powerful leader has to send out powerful messages, Fenn. Simple messages simple people understand – you know that now. A long time ago, I had more room for clemency, but..." He cocked an eyebrow ruefully at his mechanical fingers, twitching them a fraction so that the metal digits scraped against each other. "Look where that got me!"

"SIR! THE SHIP!" the Terra shouted. He pointed at the water between the *Warspite* and the estuary. Fenn heard the fear in the Terra's voice and followed the line of the Terra's finger.

Heading towards the *Warspite* was a trawler, going at such a speed it bounced on the water, frothing up two fronds of surf as high as the bowsprit. Black smoke was pluming out of the back as its engines strained. Whoever was at the helm didn't care that the trawler would burn out. Chilstone grabbed the telescope and trained it on the figure standing at the helm.

"Moray!"

"It's heading straight at us!" the Terra shouted. The ship was less than two hundred yards off. Fenn remembered Moray's final words on the matter: *leave Chilstone to me*.

Now Moray was acting on them. It was the perfect moment to destroy Chilstone; out on the high seas the

Warspite was impossible to get close to, but here – its bow already surrounded by five tugs and in the shallows – it was a sitting duck. Even without the element of surprise, the huge ship could never turn in time.

The trawler had picked up even more speed and was now only a stone's throw away. Fenn ducked between the Terra guards and ran towards the stern. He had only got to the mid-beam when a thunderous explosion knocked the wind from his lungs and the deck from beneath his feet. Clouds of acrid, wet smoke billowed into the air and rained down on them as shock waves shuddered through the ship, scattering the gulls roosting on the radar antenna. The *Warspite* listed violently as water gushed into the hole in her side, then she began to slowly tip, port-side first. The Terras on deck slid down and across the rails plunging into the sea.

Fenn was hurled against the Scragnet crane and grabbed the lowest rung of its maintenance ladder. The giant magnet had already broken free and was swinging wildly. The blast had knocked Chilstone to the ground, but he'd just managed to hook the end of his cane around one of the legs of the crane.

He's getting away again! the voice hissed in Chilstone's ear. Chilstone's face was twisted with pain as he clung onto the cane. His metal legs were useless, unable to get any purchase as they clattered and scratched on the wet iron deck.

Fenn scrambled up the ladder away from Chilstone, who was inching closer, pulling himself up his cane, fist over fist. His cowl, blackened and wet from the soot, tangled over his arms, like bats' wings. Fenn reached out and grabbed one of the struts to drag himself onto the crane's arm. The ship shuddered again and slumped deeper and Fenn slipped, clinging on desperately. There was a grinding sound from the furthest gun turret as it began to tear away from its footings. Chilstone lunged for the lowest rung.

Don't let him get away! the voice screeched, as the pain twisted through the iron pegs in his legs. Chilstone clawed up towards Fenn, dragging his legs behind him. The *Warspite* groaned as the front of her bow sheared off and began pulling the rest of the hull with her. Water began rolling up the deck towards them.

Hurt him! the voice shrieked as Chilstone slashed at Fenn's hand with his cane. Fenn howled in agony as it smashed down on his fingers. He lost his grip and nearly fell, but hooked his leg over a girder, clinging on. Chilstone's face contorted with fury as he dragged himself higher. He lifted the cane to strike again, but as he raised his arm, he felt the cane fly out of his hand towards the huge magnet as it swung past behind him. Fenn eased himself up and edged along the crane's arm.

The gun! the voice screeched frantically.

There was nowhere left for Fenn to go and he watched in horror as Chilstone unbuttoned the holster; but before he could draw it, the gun had flown from his grasp and pinned itself to the magnet as well. The ship slumped sideways as she took on more water and the magnet swung back towards the crane again. Forgetting his recent metal alterations, Chilstone tried to grab the gun back. Instantly his hand smacked against the magnet with a clang.

As he struggled to get away, he kicked out, and the straps and iron pegs in his legs also clamped tight to the magnet's underside. Fenn watched in horror, remembering the flies he used to free from the sticky spiders' webs spun in the bottles that made the kitchen window back home. The more Chilstone tried to prise himself free, the more entrapped he became. Fenn felt the same sharp lurch of pity for him as he had for the helpless flies.

The stern of the ship had lifted out of the water but now, as the ship broke into two pieces, it crashed down with a terrible crack, forcing a huge grey wave up towards the Scragnet. Fenn clutched the Scragnet's arm even tighter, trying to keep a grip in the wet. He watched wide-eyed as the sea began washing around Chilstone; no longer Fenn's enemy but just a frightened old man, snagged by his own hate, his body numbing with cold as the icy waters rose.

You failed, the voice said sorrowfully. *It's all over.*

It sounded withered and frail in Chilstone's ear before suddenly fading away altogether, leaving him with a strange new silence.

Then, for the first time in years, Chilstone heard the wind sighing over the sea and waves slopping against the hull of the sinking *Warspite*. He noticed how jagged and forlorn the gulls' cries were, how sweetly a far-off skylark was singing, and how the *Warspite*'s wire flag-hoists clattered like the noise his daughter used to make when banging pots for drums. Out of the blue, he recalled the sound of her laughter and remembered the weight of her in his arms as he lifted her to see over the *Warspite*'s rail. Then the strangest thing happened; he thought he felt her arms around his neck, holding on to him so tightly.

As a final wave swept up, Fenn desperately threw out his arm, trying to grab at Chilstone's cowl. But the sea had already swallowed him and he disappeared from view.

20

Fenn hit the water at the exact moment the *Warspite*'s last gun turret disappeared beneath the waves. It was freezing and the water was filled with thousands of bubbles. He was too weak to stop himself being dragged down through the whirlpool, almost as if the *Warspite* wanted to pull him down to her grave. But the thought of his friends and Halflin spurred him on and he swam as hard as he could through the churning waters, with no sense of up and down, until beyond the swirling murk he saw the yellow glow of daylight. He drove himself towards it, breaking through the surface, gasping for air. The sea around him was deserted.

At first his heart flipped over with fear, thinking Fathom hadn't freed the *Crescent* in time, or that somehow she'd been dragged down in the *Warspite*'s suction, but then he heard a wild, jubilant yell from far behind him. The *Crescent* was chugging towards him, safe and sound, with Fathom screaming excitedly at the bow; he had realised the tug was small enough to be pulled down with the drag of the *Warspite* and had got her a safe distance away. He threw out a buoy and Fenn clung onto it while Fathom dragged him in. As Fenn fell onto the deck, he saw Fathom's eyes were puffy – he'd been crying. Tikki squeaked and jumped somersaults with happiness as the two boys hugged, crying with relief and exhaustion.

"I thought you were dead!" Fathom's words choked out as he hitched Fenn's arm over his shoulder and lugged him into the cabin. Tikki bounced along behind them chattering with joy and pawing at Fenn's legs. Inside, Fathom unearthed a stash of hessian sacks in the cupboard and gave them to Fenn to dry off with while he stuffed the stove with logs, making the flames spit and sparkle, green and purple. He left the stove door open so the searing heat flooded the room. Fenn put his boots upside down by the grate to dry.

"You didn't pull the rope!" Fathom said. "I waited! And when I hoisted the crate up anyway, it was empty!"

He dragged Viktor's chair up to the stove and helped Fenn down into it. Tikki danced impatiently at Fenn's feet, waiting for him to be dry enough so he could jump up.

"Then some Terras spotted me so I ran for it... I'm sorry..." Fathom's voice thickened with guilt.

"We'd both have drowned if you hadn't!" Fenn said, shivering. "Anyway, I told you not to wait."

Fathom roughly rubbed the hessian sacking over Fenn's head to dry his hair. His lips were blue.

"What happened?" Fathom asked, nudging the kettle back onto the hotplate. He held one of the sacks up against the stove to warm it through and a malty smell filled the cabin as the hemp heated.

"Terras caught me," Fenn explained.

Fathom wrapped the warmed hessian around Fenn's feet; they were like ice. He kept chafing them until they turned pink.

"I'd just cast off when I heard this massive bang. I kept going to get clear, then watched her go down." Fathom swallowed hard and looked at his hands. "I thought... I..."

He couldn't say what he thought; it was too horrible to imagine.

"It was Moray," Fenn said, pulling on his shirt and reaching down for Tikki. Now that he'd stopped moving about so much, Tikki scrambled up onto his lap.

"But how?" asked Fathom.

"He had a boat hidden; packed with explosives he'd been stealing from the mines," Fenn said. "I can't believe he really did it." He looked out at the grey sea. "But if he thought I'd been killed he must have thought the Sargassons had nothing left to lose."

Fathom stood up and flipped the lid off a tin, tipping the last spoonful of black powder into a mug.

"People do crazy things when they're desperate," he said, pouring the hot water in. The water darkened to a peaty brown as the steam unfurled. "Like pretending to be someone to get a mouthful of food…" he mumbled as he watched the grains swirl. He slid Fenn a guilty glance.

Fenn put his hand on his arm. "I don't care if you pretended to be me – I'd have done the same – anyone would."

A tear of relief ran down Fathom's cheek and plopped into the drink.

"Don't cry in my coffee!' Fenn teased, poking him in the ribs.

"That's the last of it!" Fathom laughed and wiped his cuff over his cheeks.

"You, Amber … all of you … you're the best friends I ever had," Fenn said, suddenly serious.

"We're the *only* friends you ever had!" Fathom pointed out.

"True! But if I hadn't met you lot, I wouldn't be alive." Fenn passed the rest of the coffee to Fathom to finish. "Let's get back to the others."

* * *

They raced to get the *Crescent* back to the *Brimstone*, pushing her harder than she'd ever sailed, on a course set for the estuary from where the canal was cut. Both feared the worst for the prisoners on the Hellhulks, and sure enough, as they approached, they saw the *Brimstone* was ablaze; the wooden shacks that had once clustered over her sides were charred to cinders, and the surf breaking up against her red-hot hull frothed black with ash. She was deserted.

"There's no one left," Fathom said.

"Do you think they've got behind the Wall?"

Fathom shrugged, but as they bumped against the dock, they both saw the stone-yard was strewn with bodies of both Seaborns and Terras, where fighting had continued on land. As they looked more closely, though, they saw guns and truncheons lying in the dirt, and Fenn counted at least six dead Malmuts. Dozens of Terra masks had been discarded on the ground, like clots of tar. Here and there, the Terras had even discarded their jackets and ripped off Terra Firma badges, flipping over in the wind like red-and-black petals. A smile spread across Fenn's face.

"They've surrendered," he shouted as Fathom dropped the gangplank. Fenn put Tikki deep in his pocket – he was still jumpy and nervous – and as they scrambled across to the dock, Fenn heard a frantic whinnying nearby. Five cob horses were rearing up from the chains fixing them to a huge barge moored alongside. They skittered wildly on the spot, the whites of their eyes flickering. Fenn and Fathom ran over to free them.

It took some time to calm them enough to unclip the first harness, but as soon as they did, the cob shied away, rearing on its hind legs, before bolting off into the marsh. As they freed the animals, they each sprang away from the water's edge, cantering inland.

Fenn frowned. "Something's wrong," he said.

"C'mon. More Terras could be coming."

But Fenn was staring out over the water; the tide was turning, but too fast. It was flowing out towards the sea, pulling the boats away from the shoreline. The whole body of water was retreating.

Suddenly the huge barge alongside them dropped, snapping its mooring lines. In a second it was dragged back by the ferocious pull of the reverse tide and spun away into the estuary like a matchstick. As Fenn watched, the entire water levels sank downwards. It was as if all the water had just disappeared, sucked back out to sea.

"What's happening?" Fathom cried.

At that moment, something rumbled in the deep. The ground pulsed and the marsh shifted. Far below its years of layered earth and peat, there fell a single lumpen beat, like the last, dull thump of a dying heart. Beneath the sludge, something ancient broke, sloughing off the years that had silted over it.

Then out of nowhere, the manic shrieks of thousands of seagulls shattered the air. There was a sudden warm downwind, caused by beating wings, and they realised it wasn't just gulls; the air was full of every kind of bird, darkening the sky like a storm cloud over their heads, all flying in the same direction – away from the ocean.

The estuary was emptying; as the water retreated, the landscape before the last Rising revealed itself, like an old ghost. The first object to materialise was the tethering arm from one of the first Punchlocks, abandoned when the water levels rose too high for the lock to work any more. It lifted out of the sea like an accuser's blackened finger, pointing towards the hundreds of wrecked boats that had spewed from its jaws and been dragged out to sea. Their masts and the ribs of hulls stuck out from the mud like bones in a graveyard, coated with seaweed and oil spills.

Next came the old town, long lost in the first Rising. The highest and strongest buildings that had survived years of submersion rose up out of the wet: factory chimneys, a church tower with a metal cockerel still fixed to its spire. A pylon that had once brought electricity, its intricate struts ragged as rotten lace. Then a peculiar sound started, like a fluttering of hundreds of moths.

The water receded yet further and more of the town came to light: crumpled cars heaped against the edge of an old sea defence; children's swings rusted rigid. Houses gurgled and belched as the water was sucked out through their windows and doors. The fluttering reached a crescendo and Fenn saw that the brown ripples in the mud were silvered with thousands of fish, thrashing in the ooze, joined by a clackety rattle as multitudes of crabs scuttled up the banks as they tried to escape. But escape from what?

From deep in the marsh came a keening howl as a wolf called its young to the den. There was a rushing sound from out at sea and a wet, salt-filled wind blasted the gorse. The last leaves clinging to the alders by the canal's edge were stripped from the branches and a grimy rain scattered over them, quick and hard, gritty on their skin. Fathom looked at Fenn for an answer, but Fenn was white-faced. A short wave was now rolling back in towards them, bunching up in the estuary. Fathom followed Fenn's gaze.

"What's the matter?" he asked. The wave wasn't very high – nothing so serious as to make Fenn pale like that. It was already dissipating as it travelled up the channel.

"RUN!" Fenn yelled, pulling Fathom with him as he careered across the stone-yard. "RUN!"

Fathom looked back. The horizon seemed to have disappeared, as if bright blue winter sky was suddenly exactly the same colour as the grey sea. With a sickening jolt he realised he wasn't looking at the sky at all, but a colossal wave thundering towards them.

Hundred mile an hour, Halflin once said, when Fenn asked him how come more people hadn't escaped the great Rising. *Think yer'd outrun that?* Fenn realised they had no more than a minute before it hit the shore.

The boys hurtled onto the cart tracks and into the mine. Fenn wrenched a lamp from the wall as they raced down into the gloom. They reached the first big cavern where they had worked with Humber and sped across its rocky floor, skidding on loose stones and scraping themselves raw on the rough rocks. Fenn dragged Fathom up the short slope that forked into the two small caves.

"This way!" he shouted. The roaring of the wave was getting louder, amplified in the mine's dozens of tunnels and caverns.

"On the right!" Fenn just managed to gasp as they crashed past the props, dust and grit showering down on them. They stumbled down into the tiny cave by the tunnel's entrance. The loose pile of rip-rap Humber had used to disguise the opening had gone and a dark tunnel gaped. Behind them they could hear the rumble of water getting louder and nearer. Ahead they could hear the distant sound of many voices.

"There are still people in there!" Fathom yelled as he skidded down into the tunnel. At that moment there was a terrible crashing from the mine's entrance as carts, sleepers, tools and stone were swept ahead of the wave. Fenn realised Humber's tunnel had to slope down to get beneath the Wall; if the wave hit that, hundreds of people could drown. He had to block it off. Fenn grabbed Tikki and stuffed him into Fathom's arms.

"I'll catch you up!" he shouted. "Tell them to run!"

He ran back to where the rock picks and huge lump hammers rested against the mine's wall. He found the biggest hammer he could lift and dragged it to the last stanchion propping up the ceiling. He hoisted it up, nearly toppling over with the weight of it, and swung it with all his might against the oak prop. The post shuddered and Fenn was showered with dust. A tiny crack inched across the ceiling. He lifted the hammer again and lumped it against the stanchion a second time; dust and small pieces of rock scattered down on his head.

The deep grinding sound was getting deafening as the water hurtled through the passages, washing everything forwards in its path as it thundered onwards. Fenn peered into the gloom; the wave was billowing out like an explosion into the cavern below, black as smoke. As the water belched forwards, the lantern blew out and Fenn was plunged into total darkness. A huge whooshing sound filled the tunnel.

"RUN!" he hollered to Fathom, praying he could hear him. He swung the hammer one last time. The stanchion gave way and the ceiling collapsed. Instantly Fenn spun round and hurtled after Fathom. He could hear rocks falling as the water began to dislodge the barrier he'd made, then seconds later he felt a cold spurt of water on his back, as if a dam had sprung a leak. He kept running, his heart pounding, until a massive roar shuddered through the cave and the water caught up with him, smacking him in the back like a huge fist. He just had time to take one huge, final breath, then, before he could think of anything else, he was upside down in the slurry.

Digging deep inside himself, Fenn found his last reserve of strength. He kicked out against the stones stirred up in the water and swam forwards. The force of the water was buffeting him this way and that, smashing him against the tunnel's walls. There was no way he could control his body. Instead, he put his arms around his head to protect it against the tumbling rocks and stopped swimming, bunching himself up like a baby. He'd let the water take him where it wanted and trusted it not to kill him. The water swirled up and back on itself, but at last threw him into a current which surged down the tunnel.

For some reason Fenn didn't feel scared any more and

he just let himself roll with the water. He lost any sense of time, but eventually – just when he thought he couldn't hold on for another second – he hit the surface again, spluttering and gasping. The tide of water was still streaming on, but somewhere, far ahead in the distance, he briefly caught a glimpse of a hazy white light. He opened his mouth to yell to Fathom that he was OK, but before his voice had left his throat he was dragged back under by the water's currents.

Epilogue

Something warm and wet was tickling Fenn's nose and he tried to sit up, but there was a warm weight on his chest. His eyes blinked open for a second but the light was too bright and he squeezed them shut again. The warm weight on his chest was lifted away.

"Keeps doin' that! Yer gotta take it! Go play wiv it outside!"

It was his grandad's voice. Fenn opened his eyes in time to see Halflin pushing Tikki into Comfort's arms, who happily skipped off before Fenn could call her back. He pushed himself up.

"Grandad!" he cried, throwing his arms around Halflin's neck. They hugged for a long time. It felt like he'd never let go.

"Yer had me scared good 'n' proper there," Halflin

mumbled, releasing Fenn at last and helping him sit up properly, propping a pillow behind his head. Halflin's eyes were red; he'd been crying. Fenn had never seen that before.

They were at the far end of a huge whitewashed hall, lined on each side with iron beds. At the other end of the room, the huge Scotian who had fought so valiantly on the *Brimstone* was now teetering dangerously on a chair with a pail in one hand and a brush in the other; half a Terra Firma logo showed beneath the white paint dripping down the wall. Around every bed were scattered bags and clothes; some people slept, others sorted through their bedraggled possessions, a few went from bed to bed, tending wounds or bringing the injured steaming bowls of soup.

Fenn turned to look out of the window, but it was so high he couldn't see much other than stark trees, with a hard winter sun glaring through the scratches of their bare branches. A movement next to Fenn made him turn and look, and he realised Amber was curled up, fast asleep, in a big armchair next to him. She shivered in her sleep and Halflin pulled her blanket up, tucking it gently around her shoulders.

"This one never left yer side," he murmured. "Yer two other mates are kickin' around 'ere some place too. They only jus' went ter get some nosh. Leek and tater soup," he said, nodding at the old man in the next bed who was slurping from a bowl.

"And Humber...? Magpie?"

"Both knockin' about 'ere too. Most of the Seaborn got through. Just 'em Terras stuck out on the marsh. They won't 'ave made it. But them Sargassons did; the wave shrunk a bit by the time it hit 'em an' the trees slowed the water. The Wall took a hammerin' but Humber were wrong. The Seaborns built it good 'n' strong."

"What about Viktor?"

"Him too! The *Sastimos* was already out at sea when the wave came. Remember I told yer? The sea's the best place ter be if a big one comes? Shore's the worst."

"So where are we?" Fenn asked.

"*Inside!*" Halflin said. "We're *inside!*"

"You mean..."

Halflin nodded happily, hugging his knees like a child. He suddenly looked much younger. "We're on the other side of the Wall. On land! Real land!" he whispered incredulously, stomping his foot on the floor as if to prove it. "We're safe boy! Safe!" His eyes widened at the wonder of it; he'd spent his entire life expecting to drown one day.

"But what about the Terra Firma? And the Landborn?"

"Don't 'spect the Landborn will give up the Mainland too sharp, but the Terras 'ave mutinied. Most of 'em were treated bad by Chilstone, truth be told," Halflin said. "Dunno what'll 'appen with the Landborn. We'll 'ave ter see if they kick up trouble."

Fenn watched as Halflin fumbled with a tin jug on the crate by the side of his bed, filling a metal beaker with water. As he brought it to Fenn's lips to drink, his hands were trembling.

"How long have I been asleep?"

"We got yer out tha' tunnel yesterday mornin'. You must've got a whack." Halflin shook his head. "Ter think I thought yer weren't ready fer the marsh, an' yer took on the world!"

He put the beaker back on the crate, then held Fenn's hand in his own, but he wouldn't meet his eye. After a few minutes, he mumbled something inaudible into his lap.

"What's that?" Fenn asked, leaning closer to hear.

Halflin coughed and squinted up at him from under the shaggy mantelpiece of his brows. "I said … d'you hear what I tol' yer? About you an' me?" he whispered.

"All of it," Fenn said, squeezing his hand tightly. Halflin nodded, and managed a half-smile. "Don't change nothin' fer me," he said tentatively, looking down at their two hands clasped together.

"Nor me, Grandad," Fenn replied quietly.

Then Halflin's smile broke into a wide, eye-crinkling

grin. He clapped his hands together brightly.

"Look at us, boy! In Terra barracks!" he cried. "Never thought we'd get behind the Wall, let alone in the lap of luxury!" He leant close to Fenn's ear and whispered like it was a secret only he knew. "There's hot water! Comes out the taps!"

Fenn made his way down the hill towards the depot, a large brick building next to the Terra barracks they'd been staying in for the past few weeks. Two more Hellhulks had just arrived that morning and it was his turn to be on shift to make sure people had enough clothes and knew where they were supposed to go.

The barrow of logs that he and Fathom had spent all afternoon splitting, bounced and spat stones from its wheels as he trundled down the path. Tikki rode on the top, sometimes jumping off to investigate an interesting-looking bush before jumping back on to enjoy the ride and bask in the sunshine. His coat was glossy-brown now, the colour of chesnuts. Fenn swung around a bend in the path, trying to catch up with Fathom, but he was already far ahead. He seemed to have grown a foot in the last few weeks with eating well for the first time in his life. The two of them were taking the wood to the kitchens, a long, low block where all the camp's cooking was done.

"Hurry up, slowcoach!" Fathom called over his shoulder. "They've got the fires lit already!" Fenn glanced to where a grey spiral of smoke was creeping across the sky. The sun was low and the cooks would be hard at work.

Since the first Hellhulks had arrived in East Isle's southern bays, five more had docked. Now that the Terra Firma had been disbanded, there was no reason that people shouldn't make their way to West Isle or the Mainland, but East Isle remained the place where Seaborns felt they would be truly welcomed. Inland, huge stores of food had been discovered, but while the Terra Firma built Walls, they'd neglected the land they'd fought so hard to steal. Fruit had rotted in the orchards, crops withered in the fields. A group of Seaborns and Landborns had formed, and Humber was unanimously voted to lead them; they were to work out how best to use the limited land. Seaborns had made so much with so little for so long that the land offered riches beyond their dreams; they knew exactly how to make every scrap of soil work for them.

Fenn whistled to Tikki, who jumped off the barrow, then he tipped the load of wood out around the backs of the kitchens, dusted his hands down and walked quickly towards the clothing depot. As he hurried out of the woodsheds, he met Halflin and Comfort, who was hand in hand with another little girl a little younger than her.

"We jus' found this one, din't we Comfort, so we're takin' her ter Magpie fer some grub."

He signed the words as he spoke and Comfort watched him, giggling behind her hand. When he'd found out Comfort had never spoken, Halflin set about teaching her to sign. He also spent an entire evening painstakingly smoothing a round of slate and drilling a hole in it so she could wear it on a length of string, so when she got stuck she could draw or write instead.

"I'll come and find you later then, after work," Fenn smiled, ruffling Comfort's hair. He ran on to the depot; he was already late. Tikki scampered behind.

It was a huge building, where the Swampscrews had once been repaired. Inside, it still stank of diesel and was hot and noisy, with hundreds of people thronging by trestle tables, clothes piled up in their arms, extra blankets being doled out to those with young children and babies.

He quickly began weaving through the crowds, scanning for Amber or Gulper; he'd made sure he'd be working alongside them. The week before, he'd landed up with a man who wouldn't stop going on about how he'd met Fenn Demari once, and even when Fenn looked him full in the face, he still didn't stop saying how he was built like an ox and was over six feet tall. At last he spotted Amber in the far corner, crouching down, helping a little boy try on a coat.

He laughed to himself as he watched her spoil a tender moment by stuffing a hat so roughly on his head that she bent his ears down into two right angles. Some things would never change about Amber, but some things had. She looked so different now she'd had enough to eat, but Fenn could still see the sadness in her eyes.

He was pushing forward to reach her when suddenly something out of the corner of his eye distracted him. It was a woman trying to talk to a Scotian couple, but not able to make herself understood. They were queuing up to get clothes for the squabble of children, who were pinching and thumping each other by their parents feet. The woman must have already been to one of the clothing points because she was wearing one of the wool jackets salvaged from the Terra barracks and had on a huge pair of men's boots from the same place. The clothes were too big and she looked half-starved, but that wasn't uncommon to see, so Fenn couldn't work out why she'd caught his eye. At that moment there was a sudden shriek of joy from the other side of the hall, as a husband was reunited with his wife. Fenn looked away to where the couple were hugging and by the time he looked back the woman had vanished. He shrugged to himself and carried on walking but something made him stop. There was just something about her he couldn't shake off.

When he turned back again he found her silhouetted against the bright sunlight streaming through the doorway. He was suddenly struck by how lonely she looked but there was something else about her too; she seemed familiar and he wondered if he'd seen her at the Shanties. He watched her first look left, then right, as if unsure which way to go, then she darted off, surprisingly quick for someone who looked so fragile. Some instinct made him follow her. He called Tikki who jumped up into his arms.

By the time he got into the tent where the registrations were made, he had lost her again. It was even busier than the depot. Hundreds of people sat on the floor, some sleeping, but then he spotted her, carefully stepping over the sleeping bodies as she made her way to the door. He was so out of breath that when he caught up with her, all he could do was hang on her arm, panting. She looked at him distrustfully; she didn't know who he was, just that a strange boy with what looked like an otter dangling around his neck had grabbed her but couldn't speak. At last he found his voice.

"Are you looking for someone?" he asked. Her wide, grey eyes were filled with a hopeless expression.

Tikki's nose twitched inquisitively, as if he too recognised her. She was worn out and swayed slightly, her huge new boots acting like ballast for her skinniness. Instead of answering, she hugged her jacket tightly around her shoulders, her watery eyes flashing like chips of glass. But Fenn knew she wasn't going to cry, at least not in front of him; he'd seen a tiny muscle at her temple, flexing as she gritted her teeth.

"Did they tell you to go to Missing Persons?" he asked. "People are found all the time."

Fenn had now missed the start of his shift and would be in so much trouble with Amber, but he couldn't bear to leave the woman on her own. "I'll take you if you want," he offered. "This way." He pointed to the opening at the end of the tent.

She acknowledged his kindness with a little nod, so fleeting he could have missed it, and walked on, towing her sadness behind her. People glanced at her as she passed, stepping out of her way, as if her unhappiness were something black and spidery creeping out of her that they didn't want touching them.

They headed out of the tent. The sun was at its lowest before disappearing altogether and its orange rays raked the sky, dazzling them both. The tips of her long, grey hair lifted in the breeze, showing threads of reddish brown. She had been pretty once – you could see that – but she was gaunt now. She stumbled and Fenn cupped his hand beneath her frail elbow, as if he was holding something terribly fragile, like an egg. All of a sudden she began talking, confessing the guilt she carried with her grief.

"They promised me," she whispered. "They swore we'd be together. It was one of those convoy ships; I gave them *everything*. I … I keep thinking she might have thought I *wanted* to send her away…"

She faltered, and had such a look in her eyes, such a hurt, wounded look that Fenn could hardly bear it. Her face hollowed like she was biting the inside of her cheeks to stop herself crying. Fenn went to put his arm around her, but she shrugged him off. She didn't want comfort; she just wanted her child. She straightened her back, gave him a brittle smile and marched on bravely, murmuring a tune just under her breath. She had forgotten most of the words and only a few fragments trembled out.

"Hey, diddle, diddle *hm, hm, hm, hm, hm-hm, hm*, cow, jumped over *hm-hm, hm. Hm-hm, hm, hm* to see such sport and the dish ran away *hm hm hmm*." Her voice quivered with sadness, but she kept going.

At last they reached Missing Persons, a large wooden hut Fenn had helped build from driftwood. They pushed open the door and went inside. On each wall, long lists were chalked in alphabetical order, where people could log their own names and those they were searching for. There were dozens of people, but apart from the soft scraping of chalk, the tent was in complete silence. The woman started reading the first list.

"Who are you looking for?" Fenn asked again, following her gaze.

"My daughter," the woman replied. "Her name is Amber."

Fenn Halflin has only ever known a dark and flooded
world, controlled by the ruthless Terra Firma and their
cold-blooded leader, Chilstone. When he is separated
from his grandfather, Fenn's only companion is a
half-tame mongoose, Tikki.

Abandoned on the dangerous Shanties, Fenn survives
with other children living in constant fear of Chilstone
and his monstrous Fearzero ship. But Fenn's past
holds a secret – one which forces him out of
hiding to face his destiny.

Timothée de Fombelle
Vango Book One: Between Sky and Earth

Fleeing from the police and more sinister forces on his trail, Vango must race against time to prove his innocence – a journey that will take him to the farthest reaches of distant lands. Can Vango uncover the secrets of his past before everything is lost?

"Exciting, unusual and beautifully written." *David Almond*

Vango Book Two: A Prince Without a Kingdom

Vango has spent his life abandoning his loved ones to protect them from the demons of his past. But the mystery of his identity has started to unravel, and in the shadows of war and persecution, the truth will finally come to light.

"A distinctive and atmospherically cinematic tale." *Independent*

Rob Lloyd Jones

WILD BOY

London, 1841. A boy covered in hair, raised as a monster, condemned to life in a travelling freak show. A boy with an extraordinary power of observation and detection. A boy accused of murder; on the run; hungry for the truth. Ladies and Gentlemen, take your seats. The show is about to begin!

"A pacey, atmospheric and thrilling adventure." *Metro*

WILD BOY AND THE BLACK TERROR

A new sensation grips London – a poisoner who strikes without a trace. Is there a cure for the black terror? To find out, Wild Boy and Clarissa must catch the killer. Their hunt will lead them from the city's vilest slums to its grandest palaces, and to a darkness at the heart of its very highest society.

"An exhilarating read with great characters."
The Bookbag

Amanda Mitchison

MISSION TELEMARK

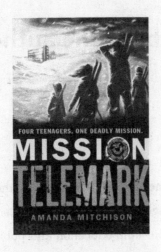

Norway, December 1942. The British government has become aware that Hitler is trying to find a way to make a nuclear weapon. Now the Allies' fate rests in the hands of four teenagers who must survive for weeks in freezing conditions before they launch a sabotage attempt that will decide the course of the war.

"A gripping, well-paced adventure." *The Daily Mail*

About the author

Francesca Armour-Chelu grew up by the Suffolk Coast. She studied English and Drama at Goldsmiths and went on to work in museum education and public libraries. Her experience of living on water meadows in an abandoned Edwardian railway carriage inspired her debut novel, *Fenn Halflin and the Fearzero*, which was short-listed for the Mslexia Children's Novel Competition 2012. Francesca lives in Suffolk.